NEW YEAR, NEW HERO

Kate Benning and Tom Cole, both members of neighbourly households known locally as The Three Families, had always known they would marry each other.

However, Tom was stifling her, and Kate was determined to free herself of these marital expectations before the New Year began.

She dreamed of getting herself a new hero in the New Year.

And a dog. She'd always wanted a dog.

But nothing ever goes according to plan...

There is a list of The Three Families' members, and a seating plan of them too, in the front of this book.

To receive advance notice of new books let me know your email address at the bottom of any of the pages on my website at: www.SusanAlison.com – or contact me direct.

Susan Alison lives in Bristol, UK, and writes and paints full-time. She paints dogs, especially Border Collies, Corgis, Whippets and Greyhounds. Every now and then she paints something that is *not* a dog just to show she's not completely under the paw – mainly, she's under the paw…

Short stories of hers (*not* usually about dogs) have been published in women's magazines worldwide.

In 2011 she was presented with the Katie Fforde Bursary Award (with which she's incredibly chuffed).

She has a dog blog (with the occasional non-dog painting) at www.MontyandRosie.blogspot.com and a website at www.SusanAlison.com and if you'd like to receive her (very occasional) newsletter in the comfort of your own inbox, there is a space to put your email address on the bottom of any page on her website.

Twitter: @bordercollies

Facebook: Susan Alison Art

SUSAN ALISON

NEW YEAR, NEW HERO

A ROMANTIC COMEDY

ACKNOWLEDGEMENTS

My special thanks go to my son for his constant encouragement, and brilliant editorial input. He's simply the best!

Any mistakes found in this book will be down to me.

As always, I acknowledge that life would be generally flatter, greyer and so much more sweetly scented and boring, without my dogs.

Cover art by Susan Alison

In Memory of the Awesomeness

that was Jeff-Dog

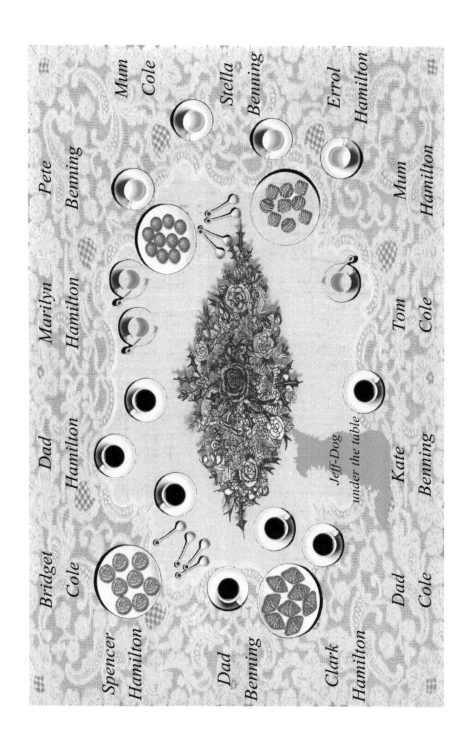

Mum
Cole

Stella
Benning

Errol
Hamilton

Pete
Benning

Mum
Hamilton

Marilyn
Hamilton

Tom
Cole

Dad
Hamilton

Jeff-Dog
under the table

Kate
Benning

Bridget
Cole

Dad
Cole

Spencer
Hamilton

Dad
Benning

Clark
Hamilton

The Three Families

Mum Benning aka Stella
Dad Benning
Pete Benning – policeman
Kate Benning – fuchsia specialist

Mum Cole – fruitilicious ice lolly maker
Dad Cole – architect
Tom Cole – accountant
Bridget Cole – half-hearted florist

Mum Hamilton – film-star fan
Dad Hamilton – surgeon
Clark Hamilton – investigative journalist
Spencer Hamilton – accountant
Errol Hamilton – warehouse-living, literary writer
Marilyn Hamilton

Newcomer: Rover

Chapter One

The bell rang again, even more insistently than last time, but Kate stayed right where she was, lurking in the darkness of her own hallway. She didn't have to answer the door if she didn't want to! This was *her* home and *her* life and *her* New Year's Eve. For once, she would do what *she* wanted to do and not what someone else wanted her to do.

Or, as in this case, she wasn't going to do what she didn't want to do. She wasn't going to answer the door.

She just wanted to be left in peace with her stinking clogged-up-head-cold, her fledgling New Year resolution list, her tin of homemade millionaire's shortbread, and her mug of hot chocolate. She wanted the naff but traditional New Year's Eve telly on in the background that she could switch off whenever she wanted.

Unlike visitors. She'd never been any good at switching off visitors. She'd always had to sit there and smile politely until her face ached, and she simply wasn't up to that now.

Oh, if only that were possible – the ability to switch off visitors. How wonderful that would be. She smiled to herself at the thought and imagined several people she'd like to be able to switch off.

Um – from talking, that was. She didn't mean it in any terminal way... Although... No! She did not mean it in any final way at all! Stop it, Kate, she admonished herself and barely prevented a giggle escaping. She was supposed to be lurking quietly, not laughing maniacally to herself!

One of the main problems with working and living in the same place was that she didn't get much time to herself.

1

And there were a couple of occasions when she really yearned for time by herself. One was when she was ill. She hated people fussing around when she felt unwell. Another was when it was New Year's Eve. So this was a double whammy. Especially as she'd never in her entire life achieved a solitary New Year's Eve.

A solitary New Year's Eve was an impossibility for a member of The Three Families – their so-far unbroken tradition being that they always spent New Year's Eve and New Year's Day evenings together.

But this year she was ill. Really, really ill. So no one could reasonably expect her to go to The Three Families New Year shindigs. So it was just typical that some importunate member of the public wanted something from the fuchsia nursery now and seemed to think they had the right to demand it. She'd shut the greenhouses and the little shed in which she took orders a couple of hours ago, at her usual time. If this person was so keen, he or she should have turned up earlier.

It did seem odd that someone would have such an urgent desire for a fuchsia on New Year's Eve, but nothing much surprised her these days.

She wasn't going to answer the door, though.

Everything was finally arranged the way she wanted it in her bedroom and she'd made a last trip downstairs to fill up her Cosy-Dog hot water bottle. That was when the onslaught on the door bell had begun.

Now she was stuck hiding in the shadows of the hall waiting for the unasked-for caller to go away. She was getting colder and colder standing there so still, which wouldn't help her get better. Surely she couldn't be seen or heard if she tiptoed slowly along and up the stairs. The glass in the front door was very thick and all gnarly and twisted. Surely they couldn't see her through it.

"Come on, Kate," she encouraged herself. She imagined she was a cat-burglar trying to escape detection from hordes of baying werewolves, and she moved like just another sinuous cat-like shadow along the hall. All she wanted in the world was to finally get upstairs, get undressed and dive into her comfy bed.

Another banging on the door reverberated through the house. Whoever was there was very determined. Not that it made any difference to her. Whoever it was had no business giving her a hard time this late on New Year's Eve. She waited a bit longer and decided they'd finally given up. Thank heaven for that! About to make a mad dash for her bedroom, she was taken aback when the banging started again, this time accompanied by shouting: "Kate! It's me! Open the door!"

Good grief! It sounded like Tom. What on earth did he think he was doing? Not that it made any difference to her. She wasn't expecting him, hadn't invited him, didn't want him. He could go away.

She dropped the cat-burglar act for that of outraged maiden, hand to throat, eyes wide with disbelief. The nerve of it! Their engagement had come to an end over three months ago and yet he still behaved not only as though it hadn't, but as though she were some kind of possession. She was so fed up with it!

Tom pounded on the door some more, and shouted some more, and then her mobile phone chirruped with an incoming text. Disbelievingly she checked it and sure enough the message was from him. It said: "Kate. Open the door. It's me."

"Bloody cheek!" she exclaimed under her breath.

There was no way while the sun still rose in the sky that she would open her door to him now so she texted back: "I'm in bed with a stinking cold!"

Well, it was *nearly* true, and would have been completely true if he hadn't turned up before she'd made it to her bedroom.

She crept further along and had reached the bottom of the stairs before her mobile announced another text. She ought to ignore it, but she couldn't. It said, "You can't be in bed at 8pm on New Year's Eve!"

Her fingers had texted back before her brain had really given it thought: "I can if I'm ill!!!"

What business of his was it anyway? If she wanted to spend New Year's Eve alone for the first time in her life, that was her affair and no one else's. It was unbelievable, this kind of intrusion. Especially from an ex.

His next text said: "I have champagne!"

Her next text said: "I'm ill in bed!"

His next: "Don't be such a party pooper!"

Hers: "I'M ILL IN BED!!!"

By this time she'd managed to sneak upstairs and was standing in her bedroom in the dark peering out of her window hoping she'd see him give up and drive away. But no such luck. The next text from him was decidedly sulky.

"Just open the door so I can give you the champagne even if you don't want me to drink it with you."

She was going to have to do it just to get rid of him. If she had any boiling oil and threw that down on him from above, that might get rid of him, but she didn't, so she'd have to open the door. Then she remembered that she was supposed to be ill in bed and yet here she was still fully dressed. Drat it! She threw off her shoes, socks, and jeans, pushed her feet into her sloppy old fuzzy dog-face slippers, pulled on her huge, balding dressing gown and ran her fingers through her hair so it stuck out at all angles even more than usual.

Reluctantly, Kate walked down the stairs.

On opening the door, she had to quickly bring her hands up to catch the bottle and bouquet of flowers as they were thrust in her face.

"There. That wasn't so difficult was it," Tom snarled.

"I was asleep! Because I'm ill."

"I go to all the trouble to make sure you're not alone on New Year's Eve and this is the thanks I get!"

"I *want* to be alone. I'm ill. I want to be in bed. Asleep. Recovering from being so ill. Because I'm ill."

"I've never not been with you on New Year's Eve before. And we've never not been at The Three Families New Year's Eve do together before, either."

"I've never been ill on New Year's Eve before. Ill. As in I'm not very well. I want to go back to bed now. Because I'm ill. Good night. And Happy New Year to you, too!"

"You'll be sorry. Everyone will think you're being very unsociable and unfriendly. How does it feel to be the one breaking our time-honoured tradition of The Three Families spending this night together?"

"The only thing I'm sorry about is that you woke me up when I was asleep. Because I'd gone to bed early. Because I'm ill!"

"Oh, have it your way!" he said, and stomped off into the night.

So then Kate felt awful. Even more awful than she felt anyway. Of course, she *should* feel awful. Tom's little display was designed to make her feel awful and it had succeeded. If she didn't fall in with what everyone else wanted then it was only right that she felt awful with guilt. And she did. So she was actually being a good girl by feeling awful. Anything else would be bad.

She dragged herself up the stairs feeling much worse than when she came down them. Reaching her bedroom she realized her hot chocolate had gone cold. But she was a bad person so she didn't deserve hot, hot chocolate, so she'd put up with cold, hot chocolate instead.

Without enough energy to finish getting undressed, Kate flopped on to the edge of her bed. It was as though what little life she'd had left had drained from her during the confrontation with Tom. At the same time she was conscious of some concern. Tom's behaviour seemed so out of character. Usually, he was such a calm, live-and-let-live kind of person. These days he appeared tense enough to break. She had asked him if there was anything she needed to know, or anything she could help with, but she'd been rebuffed.

This was largely why she could no longer tolerate being engaged to him, and she shouldn't let it get her down even more, so she forced herself to take off the rest of her clothes and she took a big bite of her millionaire's shortbread. But it had lost its flavour, and cold, hot chocolate wasn't to her taste either, no matter how hard she tried to make it so.

She crawled into bed and lay back feeling like she was a real dreg of humanity. She was such a mean person that she wanted to go to bed early when she was ill. How mean could she get? Tears started to roll down her face, making her skin itch. She was so unworthy. She deserved itchy skin.

Then the phone rang and immediately she was angry again. It would be Tom and he would be piling on the guilt trip, knowing it was working, knowing that guilt had been brainwashed into her from birth. Or it would be her mother doing the same thing. Or her so-called best friend, Bridget, Tom's sister, doing the same thing. She snatched up the phone and yelled, "I'm ill. I'm in bed. Go away!"

After a moment's silence a small voice said, "I'm so sorry. I must have the wrong number. My name is Honoraria Jamieson. I'm trying to reach Kate Benning. She has recently become a fosterer for our charity and we have a dog in need tonight. I'm so sorry to bother you especially with it being New Year's Eve, but if she's there I would be very grateful if I could speak to her."

"Ohmigod. I do apologise. I was expecting it to be someone else," Kate said. Typical! That was just typical! Just to add to her discomfort.

"Er. Yes. May I speak to Kate Benning? Is she there?" The caller persevered.

"This is her. I mean me. I'm Kate Benning. Just tell me what I have to do."

"But you're ill in bed, you said."

"Not so ill I can't rescue a dog!" Kate declared. In fact, she felt a new energy coursing through her at the thought of doing something so worthwhile. The cold seemed to recede from her head at the very idea, and the hope sparked that liberating a poor, terrified dog from the clutches of evil would make her less of a dreg of humanity. "Just tell me what I have to do and where I have to go."

Honoraria Jamieson proceeded to tell her all about some chap called Mr Wisley, and a poor dog called Rover, and where he was, the dog, and what she had to do about him. As she made notes she could feel herself taking on the persona of a Super Dog-Rescue Woman, who, against all odds was about to spring to the rescue of poor old Rover.

"I apologise again for it being New Year's Eve but this is part of the problem. This dog is going to be left alone again in that place on one of the main nights of the year when there is indiscriminate letting off of fireworks, and apparently he's already fearful of them from having spent the last couple of months there alone most of the time. We need to be grateful to Mr Wisley for calling it in. He didn't have to, and he's just waiting there for you to turn up, so we're in rather a hurry."

"I'm on it!" Kate yelled, hurling the phone down. She raced around throwing on the clothes she'd so recently thrown off. Then she considered where she was going – she was going to what she called the Badlands – an area of Bristol through which she drove with locked doors for fear of being hijacked at the traffic lights. Having taken this into consideration, she flung off her expensive jeans, donned her toughest ones; took off her earrings, although she felt naked without them, and tried, and failed, to take her engagement ring off. She had to leave it there on her finger like a beacon crying out to get her mugged. But she didn't have time to worry about it now!

She piled on layers of t-shirts, and finished off by lacing her old bovver boots onto her feet. She was going to look like she meant business. Well, she *did* mean business, of course, but she felt more apprehensive than she wanted to look. She grabbed up the dog lead she had bought in case she needed one and sprinted out of the house.

Kate dived into her trusty station wagon, which started instantly, and drove slowly down the drive and turned left. She had to take the turn with care because there was a bend in the road right beside her gateway. Straightening out the car and flicking her lights to main beam she caught sight of Tom's silver Jaguar parked opposite her driveway. There was no doubt in her mind about who it was. It was a very distinctive car and she'd seen it around way too much recently when she wasn't expecting to see it.

Shock tensed her foot on the accelerator and she swerved towards him, the car engine roaring menacingly. Clearly she saw Tom rear back in shock, his mouth open, hands splayed in an instinctively defensive gesture. The heavy dark of the night in contrast with the glare of her lights produced a primitive black and white woodcut-type picture of horror that engraved itself on her mental vision.

"Aargh!" she yelled and jerked the wheel down just in time to avoid smacking into Tom's pride and joy. He wouldn't forgive her for so much as *scratching* his super-duper Jaguar, let alone piling into it in her own, scruffy, two-ton killing machine. She'd never hear the end of it. Unless she finished him off as well. Which meant she either had to run into him and squish him, which had its attractions, or she had to miss him altogether. Better the latter as she had an important job to do tonight.

She wrenched the wheel around, whispered past his front bumper and, her heart accelerating at the same rate as the car, charged up the hill towards town.

"What the hell do you think you're doing?" she yelled as if he could hear her. "Are you spying on me, you thick-headed dimwit. It makes you a stalker. You know that don't you!"

Of course, he wasn't anything so menacing. She knew that. But on the other hand, this kind of behaviour was beyond the limit of what was acceptable from anyone, but even more so from someone who knew better and had known her all her life and knew full well how she'd react to it. He might have taken their break up hard, but that was no excuse for stalking her, behaving as though she was his chattel. She was going to have strong words with him when she had a moment.

When she wasn't out being Super Dog-Rescue-Woman.

And that was another thing, now she came to think about it. "I know you wanted me to keep quiet about us breaking up, Tom," she said to the night. "And I have done that, but I no longer think it's a good idea in any way, shape or form. It's making you think we might get back together again. Which we won't. Surely you must think we will, or you wouldn't be doing this stalking thing as if waiting for the second I come to my senses and beg for you to be my fiancé again. So I'm going to tell The Three Families tomorrow at the New Year's Day dinner get-together and then it'll be done, and we can move on."

She could hear him in her mind saying, "Oh no! Don't do that. It'll upset everyone."

And she would say, "Not doing so is upsetting me." She would say it firmly and that would be that.

Then the picture of his recent shock flashed in front of her eyes and she started to laugh. He'd really thought she was going to pile into him. She'd thought so too for a second so she couldn't blame him. She wondered if he'd been more frightened for himself, the unassailable Tom Cole, or for his highly polished and pampered, ultra-sensitive car. She laughed again. She ought to be sorry he'd got such a fright, but she wasn't in the least. It served him right!

Chapter Two

It was just as well she'd been too ill to go to the traditional Three Families New Year's Eve party, and that she and Tom had spent all that time in a stand-off about it when he was at her door when he shouldn't have been, or she wouldn't have been able to rescue a dog tonight. She'd have been over the limit for driving by now and she'd be doing something much less important – like drinking too much champagne and singing 'Auld Lang Syne' off key along with kilt-wearing people on the telly.

Rescuing a dog from the Badlands was so much more satisfying, even if a load more frightening.

Becoming a fosterer for a local dog charity had been a spur of the moment decision after Kate read an article citing the appalling figures on the number of dogs abandoned over the Christmas season. Apparently, the festive spirit and peace on earth ideas didn't extend to all creatures great and small. A lot of people were only interested in getting new models and chucking out the old ones.

In an unguarded moment she had mentioned her plans to Tom and hadn't received the unqualified approval that she'd hoped for. So she hadn't mentioned it to anyone else. She was just going to do it whether they liked it or not!

With the help of her sat nav she located the address the dog charity had given her. She parked as close to it as she could in case she had to make a speedy getaway. She also gave herself a quick lecture to stop the gory pictures chasing through her head caused by over-imagining possible outcomes of the looming confrontation.

She realised she was thinking incorrectly about this Mr Wisley. This was a member of the public doing his best for a poor, abandoned dog. That was better! She would be suitably grateful. Yes, she would!

Her mobile beeped, but it was probably just going to be a New Year's Eve message, and she had more important things to do, so she switched it off. But maybe she'd need her phone if there was an emergency. After all, she didn't know what this Mr Wisley bloke was going to be like. She switched it back on, but turned it to silent. Whilst doing so a message came up on screen.

It was from Tom: "I thought you were supposed to be too ill to leave your bed!!!"

This enraged Kate so much she deleted it, leapt out of the car, slammed the door and stamped up the garden path knowing that with this much rage boiling around inside her, she could face anything.

As she approached the front door it swung open, a man reached out, grabbed her arm and before she could react, pulled her over the threshold, crashing the door into its frame behind her. Then he dropped her arm as though it had burnt him.

"Uh," she managed, taken aback at this somewhat unconventional welcome. "I take it you're Mr Wisley? I'm Kate Benning, and I'm here for Rover." She stepped back from him, trying hard to appear unmoved by his odd behaviour.

"I know who you are," the man replied. "I wanted to get you inside before you rang the bell. That bastard dog goes mad when he hears the bell. He can't be controlled."

"Oh. Um. What do you mean – mad, exactly?"

"You'll see," he said grimly, and marched down the dark hallway, Kate scurrying behind him to keep up. He flung a door open into a heavily carpeted lounge. Kate barely made it into the room before a black and white blur of movement hit her full in the chest and screamed into her face.

She fell back. Luckily the door frame stopped her from falling right over backwards, but that was a dubious advantage because it also meant she couldn't get away from the dog.

His paws on her shoulders, he screamed and screamed at her. Although she could admire the beautifully perfect, strong-looking, HUGE, white teeth centimetres from her face, Kate was more scared than she could ever remember being in her life.

At the same time she could clearly hear Rover's own fear. His desperate shrieks begged Kate not to go away and leave him alone and lonely in an empty house with fireworks going off all the time, interspersed with other torments dreamed up especially to scare dogs to death.

Kate's instinct was to back away. Instead, she stepped forward and put her arms right around him. She held onto his heaving body and hugged him hard. Gradually his screams lessened and he quietened enough for her to place his front paws on the ground and for him to stay there looking up at her, whimpering, out of breath and shuddering in great draughts of air.

"See," Mr Wisley said. "Told you he was mad."

Kate stared at him in disbelief. "I gather he's been left on his own for two months since his previous owner died. Right over firework season. What do you expect?"

Mr Wisley's face hardened and Kate was struck by his small eyes, pointy nose, and his resemblance to some kind of weaselish animal. She also reminded herself that she wasn't supposed to get into discussion with him. She was only there to fill out the paperwork and leave with the dog.

Weasel-Face's glance flickered slightly but not much. He didn't care. "We gave him food," he said in a tone of voice that indicated there was nothing else required to keep a dog happy and healthy and in its right mind.

"Why didn't you call us earlier?" Kate didn't want to keep on being aggressive with Weasel-Face but she couldn't seem to help herself.

"We're busy people."

"Of course," she said, gritting her teeth and pulling out her pen and the charity's forms that needed filling out. She sat down on a ratty old sofa by a coffee table and grabbed Rover's collar to stop him climbing on her. She needed to get the formalities over and done with. "We'd better deal with the paperwork so I don't have to keep you any longer." *And so I can get this poor old dog away from this awful place and this Weasel-Faced git.*

"I don't expect you to judge me, you sanctimonious bitch," Weasel-Face said as though he could hear her thoughts. "In fact, I've changed my mind. He's *my* dog. I can do what I want with him. For example, I don't think he's been here long enough. He needs to learn more about who's in control." He gave Kate a tight little smile of triumph.

Her heart squinched itself up and blood rushed out of it too fast. She had to get herself together and be more placatory. If she had to leave without Rover, what would happen to him?

She forced her face into what she imagined might be a gentle, soothing, non-judgemental expression. "I'm so sorry. I wasn't judging you at all. I know you're very busy, that's all. And I didn't want to get in your way too much." She wondered if that would fix it or whether she'd gone too far into *'I'm just a pathetic, subservient, do-gooding female'* mode. She kept her gaze pinned firmly to the bit of his forehead between his eyebrows so she didn't have to see his whole Weasel-Face and especially not his reptile eyes and pointy nose. "And I'm aware that I might not be the fastest fosterer," she continued. "Because this is the first time I've done this so I'm still learning the ropes." She brightened her smile and clenched her hand even harder on Rover's collar. He tried to get his chin far enough back to swipe a lick at her knuckles. She would die before she left this dog here.

Or someone else would.

"Give me the papers," he commanded, and Kate wilted in relief that he'd accepted her act. Pulling herself together she whipped through everything very, very fast, snapped the lead she'd brought for Rover onto his collar and headed for the door.

"Not so fast," Weasel-Face said. He was right behind her. Somehow he'd managed to creep up on her; she could feel his breath on the back of her neck as she struggled to open the front door. She finally got the various locks in the right place, pulled the door towards her and stepped outside, Rover glued to the back of her legs. But Weasel-Face was still talking. "I've decided I want some money for him. I'm sure he's a valuable dog. You can tell he's pure-bred. And you obviously want him a lot. It must be for some reason. So you might as well pay for him."

She couldn't afford to tell him she wanted this dog simply in order to get him away from here. It wouldn't go down too well if Weasel-Face knew what she thought of him and the way he'd treated this dog. The charity had told her that it wasn't for her to judge anyone. Why not? This weasel-faced sub-human type shouldn't even be allowed to breathe the same air as a dog, let alone have one in his power. She said nothing.

"Two hundred quid," Weasel-Face stated. "You can have him for two hundred quid. That's a fair price." He reached out and grabbed Rover's lead, but Kate wouldn't let it go. Staring at him, many thoughts and words battled for dominance, but she knew she had to play it cool, had to use her brain and not her emotions if she were to win this one.

"You're the one who applied to the charity to have your dog taken away without it costing you anything. You're the one who called the charity wanting help. You didn't say anything about *selling* your dog to the charity. If you had, they wouldn't have taken it any further, Mr Weas... Wisley."

"Yeah. I was just doing the guys a favour. Clearing up a loose end. So what?"

"What guys? I thought Rover's owner had been an old lady."

For the first time Weasel-Face looked disconcerted. "Uh. Yeah. It was. My aunt. But since then, you know, there's been people looking in on him. Anyway. Yeah. Two

14

hundred quid and he's yours." He beamed at her as if he could smell victory in the air. "I can see how much you want this dog. So you can have him. For my price."

"No, Mr Wisley. No money will be changing hands here. It's illegal in this situation." She had no idea about the legality or otherwise of this situation.

Weasel-Face wasn't impressed. "You can't have him, then," he said, and snatched the lead out of her hand.

Rover stared at her. He knew she wasn't going to leave him there awash in loneliness and terrorised by fireworks. He knew she would rescue him from this situation, whatever it took.

Kate had no choice but to live up to his faith in her.

The woman from the charity had told her that they always expressed gratitude to people who handed their dogs in – better that than the dogs suffered any more than they had to. But there'd been no words of wisdom to prepare Kate for this particular scenario.

She had no money on her. Even if she had, she had no idea what the position was, given that she was here representing the charity.

That was it! Of course! She could simply represent herself instead.

"I'll give you a hundred quid for him," she said. "But it's me giving it to you, not the charity. And I don't have it on me either. I'll have to go and get it and bring it back."

"I'm not letting you out of my sight," Weasel-Face said. "You'll go away and not come back and I'll be hanging around here wasting my time. I'll come with you."

"You can't come with me. I'm not letting someone I don't know into my car with me."

"You're here with me on your own," he said if scoring a telling point.

"This is different. In my car with me driving is different. I'm not doing it." She'd be an idiot to do it. With her having to drive he'd be completely in control.

"Well, you can't go on your own. You won't come back. I know your sort. Unreliable. And it's two hundred quid. Not one hundred."

"There's no other way of getting you the money," she said, desperately hoping she wasn't crossing some legal line with the charity. Not that she'd signed anything with them. They were quite a new outfit and she'd been surprised herself at the lack of paperwork and also at how fast after she'd been inducted into the organisation she'd been sent out for a dog. She barely knew what she was doing.

"No money, no dog," Weasel said. "I don't believe you'll come back, so you can forget it."

It took everything she had, but Kate finally managed to turn away from Rover's stare. Her one idea to offer money on her own behalf had failed miserably and she was fresh out of other ideas. "That's not the way the charity works, Mr Wisley," she said. She forced herself to walk down the garden path, Weasel-Face and Rover standing in the doorway as though seeing a guest out.

The patch on the back of her legs where a dog had so recently been glued burned with an iciness she knew would never leave her.

She could not bring herself to look at Rover. She knew he would be reproaching her and begging her not to leave him behind.

So, because she was unworthy and deserved all the guilt in the world to keep her awake forever, she made herself look at him. That was her mistake.

The kindness in Rover's eyes and the slow wagging of his tail as if he understood her difficulty, broke her. She turned sharply away and walked as fast as she could to her car, managing to hold herself together until she'd started the engine and driven around the corner.

Then she had to pull into the side of the road and stop the car because her grief at letting Rover down was too great to ignore. Tears sheeted down her face obscuring her vision. She hammered the steering wheel with her fists. There had to be something she could do. There had to be! She could *not* leave Rover behind.

Making herself think calmly Kate decided to stop considering the charity. She didn't know enough about the ramifications of her actions to worry about it. She could only choose to act completely outside of it, on her own behalf as a concerned citizen. If she did that, she couldn't see that the charity, or anyone else, would have any right to say anything about it. It was none of their business.

She would, therefore, go to a cash point, draw out two hundred pounds, go back to the house and give it to Weasel-Face and leave with the dog, having bought him fair and square. No one could object to that. She was an adult, she had the right to vote, she paid all her own bills and if she wanted to buy a dog then that was her affair.

Decision made, she straightened up, started the car and shot off down the road. Then she jumped on the brakes and continued along at a more leisurely pace. She didn't need to be caught for speeding tonight. Not before she'd got Rover anyway.

Unfortunately, she didn't know this part of town and she certainly didn't feel safe enough in it to go to a hole in the wall in the middle of the night thereby presenting her back to any mugger who happened to be passing by when it was obvious she was getting cash out.   In   fact,   she never used cash points. She'd never understood why anyone did. Talk about asking for trouble. It must be a mugger's dream. But this time she had no choice, so she drove to a part of town she knew a bit better, found a cash machine in a supermarket wall and withdrew the money, feeling incredibly vulnerable and jumpy the whole time.

Driving back to Rover's House of Hell she parked as close as she could get and opened the tailgate ready for Rover to jump in so there'd be no delay in their departure. She guessed that he wouldn't be safe if he was allowed to roll around loose on the back seat so he'd better go in the boot. All prepared for a speedy getaway, she marched up the path totally ready to deal with Weasel-Face. Totally!

As she reached the front door an eerie lament of despair shivered the night air. It pierced her heart and brought her to a halt, mortal fear icing her veins. It sounded like lost souls flooding the universe with grief.

Gradually she realised, as the unearthly sound soared into the night and fell to the earth only to rise to the skies again, that what she was hearing was the sound of a dog crying its loneliness to the heavens.

Rover!

Did he expect someone to answer, or had he given up all hope that they would?

Kate fell on the door, banging on the plastic-like wood, kicking it and yelling incoherently. But there was no human reply.

There was, however, a frenzied snuffling punctuated with high-pitched yelps of excitement and the sound of a body hurling itself at the other side of the door.

Weasel-Face must have gone and left Rover behind on his own. Kate was never going to leave him again! Never. At least he knew she'd come back for him.

But she wasn't doing very well getting in to him. She ran around the property, trying all the windows that she could reach, but with no luck. Nothing had been left open or even ajar.

She'd have to try a different tactic. In the garden she found a rock, but trying to smash a window with it proved much more difficult that she'd have thought possible. The rock kept bouncing off the glass.

For a Super Dog-Rescuer Woman she obviously had a lot to learn.

Goodness knows what the window was made of, or maybe she wasn't hitting it hard enough. She *was* holding back a little, afraid to make too much noise. There was also the thought that if she broke the window with too much force the glass might explode outwards and a shard of it would leap out and sever her jugular vein and she'd bleed to death and then Rover would never be rescued.

She could see it all now – the local newspapers would read: ***Kate Benning, twenty-three-year-old fuchsia specialist nurserywoman found dead in garden with throat cut.***

Kate Benning is the youngest member of what is known locally as 'The Three Families' which comprise the families of the Bennings, the Coles and the Hamiltons. The Three Families have lived in adjoining houses for the last thirty years and are well known for their commitment to the community.

Kate Benning leaves behind loving parents, Stella and William Benning; her brother, twenty-nine year old policeman, Peter Benning; and her fiancé, Tom Cole, twenty-eight year old accountant of the firm Cole and Hamilton.

There is no definitive theory as yet for this terrible tragedy. It does look like she was trying to break into the house, inside of which a dog was found, a Border Collie called Rover. He had no comment to make, other than a despairing whimper.

Our theory, until we know otherwise, is that she was trying to rescue the dog in the age-old way of The Three Families always trying to help those worse off than themselves.

Of course, it would have to be Clark Hamilton, the eldest of the Hamilton boys, half-brother to the other two, who wrote up the report, him being an investigative journalist as he was. Although he would probably find such local items beneath him. He was usually to be found in the world's hotspots rather than in the murkier areas of Bristol.

But maybe, because it was her, he might write it up anyway. She'd often wondered if he might have a soft spot for her, and sometimes had found herself imagining what he'd be like, romantically speaking.

Of the four younger generation males in The Three Families – not counting her brother, Pete, of course – Clark was the dashing personality easily capable of holding his own with his swashbuckling film star namesake in her overwrought adolescent dreaming, even though she'd always known that Tom was the one for her. Well, until a few months ago he had been...

And, because no one knew she and Tom had broken off their engagement, it would be reported as if she was still his fiancée. Which was very annoying indeed! Even though she'd be dead at that point, it was still annoying to think of it now.

To get back to the matter in hand, Kate found herself marvelling at how people did this job of breaking in. The rock was making no difference at all. And anyway she didn't want to cut her own jugular.

A glint of moonlight on her engagement ring made her wonder if it would be possible to cut the glass tidily with the diamond, remove the piece of glass and get her hand inside to the latch and simply open the window. But no, diamonds were supposed to be very hard, but what if she ruined the ring just when she had every intention of giving it back. That wouldn't be playing fair would it?

She cast around looking for something else to try, and pounced on a length of metal lying in the weeds. Surely she could lever a window open with this. And that would be a much better bet because she wouldn't actually be breaking anything. So maybe it would be less illegal and she wouldn't feel so guilty about it.

She stuck it under the edge of the frame and leant on it. It immediately bent out of shape. Drat! On further investigation she found the putty to be loose and flaky so Kate placed the end of the metal strip in it and started to gently lever away at the edge of the glass itself. Rover helped her from inside by running up and down, leaping up at the window and generally cheering her on with woofs and yelps of encouragement. He knew her mission tonight was to rescue him. Kate knew she and Rover had developed an unbreakable bond already.

When a hand came down on her shoulder a feeling of such great fear enveloped her that she finally understood that thing where people say their limbs turned to water. She couldn't have moved if she'd wanted to. She merely froze in place staring in at Rover who had also stopped moving and stared out at her. Even his tail was motionless. Their noses would have touched if not for the glass in between.

"'Ello, 'ello, 'ello. What's goin' on 'ere then?" a voice whispered in her ear, and then completely spoilt the effect by adding, "I've always wanted to say that!"

The paralysing terror left her as fast as it had arrived. Kate whipped around to see who had caught her in the act of breaking in to steal a dog, but in the dark could make out nothing except that he was quite a bit taller than her, dressed all in dark colours and appeared to have a balaclava obscuring his face.

Did she know him? Given the facetious way he'd addressed her, having caught her trying to break into someone's property, either she knew him or he was a bit weird. On the other hand, Kate did know some weird people, too. But she couldn't think who it could be.

Not that she was that worried about identifying him because as she stared at his balaclava, a picture superimposed itself on him of a black silk mask, and that sort of hat, the one with a flat brim that chivalrous, devil-may-care heroes wore, also a black cloak flowing from his shoulders. He was every girl's dream. Zorro. Or maybe the Scarlet Pimpernel. No – it had to be Zorro. On his black horse. Hmmm. Forget the horse. Zorro. A hero. A hero who would always be there when she needed him. A dashing hero to defend the people of the land against tyranny and injustice.

The question was – had he turned up to defend her, or to defend the world *against* her?

"I'm waiting," he whispered.

"Uh, well, I'm… Well, I'm…"

"Trying to break in by the looks of things, and not doing very well. Am I right?"

"Uh. Yes. Something like that." Conversationally speaking she didn't feel at her best in the current situation.

"You're going about it in a very inefficient way if you don't mind me saying so," Zorro said.

"Oh, well. I'm not very practised," Kate mumbled. "What would you suggest?" She dropped the metal strip as though she didn't know how *that* had got in her hand, and scratched herself hard on her arm, both to give herself a more casual air, and to make sure that she was actually conscious. She didn't *feel* very conscious standing in the middle of the Badlands in the dark of night having a bizarre conversation with Zorro, her hero, about breaking and entering while a dog waited on the other side of the window for her to rescue him.

"Best thing is to let me do it for you," Zorro said. "I can do it so it doesn't look like it's been done."

"Really? Gosh. How will you do that?" You're my hero, she thought, gazing in what she hoped was the right direction. It was so murky out here she couldn't be certain which bit of him she was staring at. A sudden heat disturbed her as she realised she could be staring at anything. Hastily, she looked away.

"For a start, you can't watch what I do," Zorro said. He was still whispering. "I don't want you picking up any bad habits. Also, what you don't know you can't tell. Why were you trying to break in anyway?"

"I want that dog," Kate said, pointing in at the object of the exercise. Rover's head was tilted to the side as he tried to work out what was going on now. He wagged his tail as his rescuers both peered in at him. Kate could see the white tip of it moving in the air behind the rest of his body which was all black apart from a startlingly white ruff.

"He's been left alone in here for the last couple of months over firework season and he's terrified of them now, the fireworks, and he's lonely, and Weasel-Face demanded money and I would have paid him but I didn't have any and I went to get some, but now he's gone and I can't leave Rover in there for another night on his own. I just can't." She was getting used to being breathless.

"Weasel-Face? No, I'm not asking. It's a handy mission, though," Zorro whispered. "It gets the dog out of my way, too. Hang on." And he disappeared.

Kate wondered what he'd meant by getting the dog out of his way but was more concerned about keeping eye contact with Rover, so she stayed where she was, looking in the window. She didn't want everyone to disappear from Rover's view and make him think he'd been abandoned again. But as she gazed in to the murkiness within, his doggy face disappeared from her view and she could just see the tip of his tail moving away from her into a deeper darkness, presumably out of the room.

Zorro must have got in. That was quick! Kate stumbled around the house and was in time for Rover to run out of the front door and leap into her arms in true dramatic rescue style, except he was way too big for her and she staggered back quite a few paces desperately trying to remain upright. Rover thought this was a game and kept up with her, his front paws on her chest, his laughing face in hers, doggy breath anaesthetising away any pain.

Then Zorro was there, behind her, bringing them to a halt, grinning as though she'd provided him with some entertainment. Which maybe she had, but she didn't feel entertaining. She was very conscious of his body behind her stopping her from falling over, which somehow made her feel secure and loved and thrilled, too, even though she hadn't the faintest idea who he was. Apart from being her hero.

She also felt criminal. After all, she was stealing a dog.

"Thank you so much," she said. "How can I repay you?"

"You're very welcome," he whispered. "You can repay me by not reporting me to the police. Or anyone else, come to that. It'll be our secret. Go home and forget this ever happened. Good bye." And he held out his hand which she now noticed was gloved. She took it and they shook as though on a deal.

"Oh, and it would be a good idea if you could disguise the dog," Zorro said. "He might be on wanted posters for a while."

"Uh. How does one disguise a dog?"

"I haven't disguised a dog before, but if I needed to, I might shave his fur off, dye him, give him cheek pads, give him a mask, or maybe a costume. People dress their dogs up in all sorts of paraphernalia. I'm sure you'll think of something."

"Okay," she said, a mite feebly. How the hell was she going to disguise this dog?

She headed off, anxious now to leave the scene of the crime. Also anxious to leave Zorro before she threw herself into his arms, much like Rover had hurled himself into hers, and begged him to keep her with him, safe forever.

What was wrong with her, for Pete's sake? Yearning after some sort of outlaw as though she was in a happy-ever-after film.

Rover jumped in to the boot of the car without a backward glance. Determined not to look back either, Kate slammed the tailgate after him, got in to the driver's seat, switched on the engine and drove off into the night.

With her dog.

And her hero lodged firmly in her mind.

She didn't need to look back for one last glance at her hero's face; not that she could have seen further than the balaclava, anyway – here she was, driving along, trying to concentrate on the road, and all she could see in her headlights was Zorro.

In an effort to see the road and not him everywhere she looked, Kate flicked her eyes side to side as if to dash Zorro from her mental screen. In doing so she caught a movement in the rear view mirror that she didn't expect to see.

And there was only one explanation for it! Weasel-Face must have been ahead of her all along, and she'd made it easy for him by leaving her car open when she went to collect Rover. Thinking about it now, she couldn't believe she'd left it so vulnerable to intruders all that time, especially in the Badlands. Honestly, she deserved any trouble she now got because of her stupidity! Her fingers gripped the steering wheel so tightly they felt as though they would crack.

She'd certainly given him plenty of time to make himself comfortable in her station wagon. She must have been messing about trying to break into Rover's House of Hell for ages. Not to mention all the time she and Zorro had been discussing breaking in, and then how to disguise a stolen dog.

She continued to drive as if she didn't know he was there. Desperately she tried to think how to deal with the situation she found herself in. What did Weasel-Face have on her? Did he have a knife in his hand, ready to strike, or was he sitting in the back seat, a gun aimed at her head? Her trembling affected her limbs so badly she had to slow right down. She kept glancing at the rear view mirror trying to make out his features in the darkness behind her but all she could see was a dark mass and the merest glint of an eye. She couldn't stare for too long for fear of driving off the road.

The tension built and built until she finally blurted, "What do you want? What do you want from me? If it's the money you wanted – I've got the money. You can have it. I meant for you to have it anyway. What have you done with Rover? Why is he so quiet? If you've killed him you can forget the money." She thought she shouldn't have said that last bit. She should be conciliatory, not aggressive.

But no one answered her.

Where was her hero when she needed him?

Kate drove slowly. She felt sick imagining Rover lying in a pool of his own blood in the back, murdered because she'd been so careless about leaving her car open to all and sundry. Murdered because she'd come into his life. He'd still be alive if she'd never come out on New Year's Eve to rescue him. Ha! Some rescue. That poor old dog.

Upset though she was, she was still thinking coherently enough to realise it wouldn't be a good idea to drive home thereby showing Weasel-Face where she lived. So she took the wrong road, and then another wrong road, and waited to see what he would do next.

All the time she was trying to work out how to get out of this mess. If she stopped the car and tried to fight it out he'd have the advantage of superior size and strength straight off. It was unnerving, this silence. Why didn't he talk; make his demands known? Why did he have to put her through this torture as well? It was unreasonable and unnecessary. He must already know she was terrified of him and what he might do to Rover, not to mention to her. He must know he had the upper hand and could do virtually anything he wanted.

The thought maddened her so much that, without thinking it through, she stamped on the accelerator. The car, after an initial shriek of outrage, surged down the road as though taking off from Cape Canaveral, and then, once it was rocketing along, Kate just as suddenly stamped on the brakes bringing the car to a screechy halt.

The force of the momentum threw Weasel-Face onto the back of her neck, his breath rasping explosively in her ear, his yelp sharp with surprise.

Kate, ready to fight back, was struck with the feeling of fur and the general aroma of dog. "Rover?" she said, relief making her voice squeaky. "What were you doing on the back seat? You're supposed to be in the boot! The boot's where dogs belong." She grabbed the fur on either side of his face and brought her nose up to his. "You frightened the life out of me! I thought you were Weasel-Face." Her heart was knocking wildly on the inside of her chest and she had to take several deep breaths before it would calm down.

Rover stared very hard into her eyes, his brain obviously trying to translate her words into Dog. He decided she was inviting him even further forward and scrambled into the front passenger seat. She locked the doors and knew there was no way she was getting out of the safety of her car to make the dog get into the boot again. Sighing mightily she leaned across him, pulled the seat-belt around him and clicked it into place. He took the opportunity to swipe at her ear with his tongue.

Then she set off for home, exhausted with the tensions of the evening, cross that her hero hadn't appeared when she needed him. Even though it turned out that she hadn't needed him at all.

What had happened to her that suddenly she'd become someone who broke into other people's houses and stole their dogs? Not to mention the aggression that had flooded her system and made her stomp on the accelerator and then on the brakes knowing it would send someone through the windscreen? Even though it hadn't. Where had that streak of violence come from? None of it helped by her already fertile imagination becoming so overactive it was speeding out of control.

Although it had turned out to be Rover holding her to ransom from the back seat, and not Weasel-Face, Kate still drove home via a very circuitous route, frequently going the wrong way and driving around odd places to see if anyone was tailing her, and to lose them if they were, so they didn't know where she lived.

She could already see what life was going to be like having to live with the knowledge of her crimes. She'd always been familiar with the Guilty Conscience thing. In fact, she'd been brought up with a very healthy Guilty Conscience, but now she'd added real crime to the score, she wasn't sure how she was going to manage to live anything approaching a normal life ever again.

Chapter Three

Reaching home she was pleased to see no lights in the other half of the house. Of course, she should have known there wouldn't be because Bridget Cole, Tom's sister and her house sharer, best friend since childhood, would be at The Three Families New Year's Eve bash. On being told earlier in the day that Kate was too ill to venture forth this evening, Bridget had grandly informed her that *she* would never miss it, even if she had a raging case of leprosy plus three broken legs.

That reminded her that her phone must still be on silent. There was bound to be a load more messages nagging her to stop using illness as an excuse and to turn up to The Three Families party. Once inside her flat, on the off chance that someone might actually want to wish her a 'Happy New Year' she checked her messages.

Skimming through them, apart from a few seasonal messages from people outside The Three Families, they were mainly from a Hamilton, a Cole or a Benning wondering where she was. Considering she had rung home hours earlier to say she couldn't make it this year because she wasn't well, she didn't really appreciate any of them niggling at her to turn up regardless.

And she certainly had more urgent things to deal with at the moment, too. Zorro had said to disguise Rover. She tried to think back to that hurried conversation and remember what he'd suggested. He'd thought of a few things. As a modern day hero he must disguise himself all the time so he

28

could go riding around rescuing damsels and dogs in distress so it wouldn't be an odd thing for him.

But she wasn't so sure about disguising a dog. Give him cheek pads? She wasn't even certain what they were although she had a suspicion they were pads of some material that you put inside the cheeks in your mouth to change the shape of your face. Eyeing Rover she doubted that was a practical solution.

Hmmm. What about shaving him? He did have very thick fur. He might like to lose it for a while. Surely he must get too hot in that coat. Not that the middle of winter was a good time to try it. She rubbed her hand back and forth along his side as he lay there, much to his delight. It looked like a double coat. Would it cause him health problems if she did shave it off? She couldn't imagine being able to do it with any finesse, even if it was a good idea, which she wasn't convinced was the case. He'd probably end up with little bits of bog paper sticking to him where she'd nicked him, and tufty bits of fur sticking out where she'd missed. No, that sounded like a really bad idea!

A rash of fireworks went off and stopped Kate's considerations. Rover, the whites of his eyes showing, screamed, leapt for her and stuck his head in her armpit. Pulling him out so she could get around her flat she put on every noise-maker she possessed which produced quite a cacophony of sounds given they were all tuned to different radio and TV stations. But it did the trick. Kate, listening for them, heard more fireworks, but Rover seemed placated – or deafened – by the racket and lay down again, panting slightly after his fright.

Getting back to the problem at hand, Kate decided the best plan was to dye him, or at least his white bits. She was pretty sure that Border Collies sometimes came in brown and she booted up her computer to check online. Yes, tricolour Border Collies seemed to be quite the thing. They had brown bits on their faces and legs. She wasn't keen on dyeing his face and getting dye too near his eyes, but she could do some of the white bits on his legs and worry about doing something about his head afterwards.

A strategy in place, she rummaged through the bathroom cabinet until she found a box of hair colour that Bridget had bought for her. Bridget had wanted Kate to have the same caramelly-reddish colour as her own, but Kate had baulked at having her hair the same colour as her friend's.

It was one thing when you were six to wear the same dress, but quite another when you were in your twenties to wear the same hair.

It was around this time that Kate started to wonder why they'd been friends for so long and whether it was just habit. Bridget had got quite sniffy when Kate had decided against matching her hair colour to her friend's, but it was worth it now she needed to dye a stolen dog.

Bridget's hair was exactly the same colour as some of the dogs' legs Kate had spotted on the internet. That was handy! Kate laughed aloud imagining Bridget's annoyance if she found out her hair was dogs' legs colour. Following the instructions very carefully Kate applied the dye to Rover as he lay there, flat out on the bathroom floor. He wasn't worried. He wagged his tail a few times and then went back to snoozing again. It must be exhausting getting stolen and disguised.

Kate realized how lucky she was that he was content to merely lie there while his legs were cooking – he could so easily be up and about decorating the entire house with Rich Praline and Caramel Light Chestnut hair dye. She hadn't thought it through enough or she'd have made him get in the bath before applying the dye. She'd know for next time she needed to camouflage a dog.

Waiting for the designated time to go by she considered how she could disguise his head. It didn't help that he was such a striking looking dog. Even with his legs a different colour, Kate had to do something about his head and face to throw people off the scent.

Her thoughts wandered back to Zorro. He was effectively disguised. She had no idea who he was. But with him she didn't know if she would know who he was even if he had no mask on. She didn't know if he was a complete stranger to her or not.

Ah ha! A balaclava – a mask, in effect. She rushed out to the sitting room and grabbed her knitting bag. She had some brown wool and all the necessary gear from her (failed) attempts to knit a Fair Isle jumper. She should be able to make up a balaclava for her dog. And while she was at it she could put in thicker bits to go over his ears to at least muffle the sounds of fireworks and thunder and whatever other noises that might frighten him. What a great idea!

It took a little while and a few fumbled efforts, but in the end Kate was pleased with the result. When she tried it on Rover he looked pleased, too. Well, Kate hoped it was his pleased face he was showing her, but she was beginning to think that this dog would be happy about anything.

Except being left on his own.

And fireworks.

He looked just like Princess Leia from Star Wars. The resemblance was startling, except for the four legs, thick dark fur and tail, but these things could be overlooked.

Kate jumped as the landline phone rang. It was after three in the morning – surely a bit late, even for hardened revellers. She turned down the volume on the TV, the radios, and the CD player, shut the door so the noise from the other rooms wasn't so obvious, and answered her telephone.

"It's Honoraria Jamieson. From the dog charity. I'm outside your door. I've been here for a while ringing your bell but you're not answering. Please let me in."

Kate's stomach jittered alarmingly. This had to mean trouble! "Um. I'm sorry to have to say it, but it's a bit late for social calls isn't it?"

"It's not a social call."

This didn't sound good. Dragging her feet, but knowing she had to do it, Kate headed downstairs. Rover followed so close behind her he was in danger of pushing her the rest of the way. Reaching the ground floor, she opened her front door to Honoraria.

"Er. Sorry to repeat myself, but it *is* a bit late to be calling on people," Kate said. She felt obliged to put off what she thought must be a rapidly approaching evil hour.

Honoraria was not to be put off, however. "It's not too late for me to have to take enraged phone calls from members of the public accusing one of our fosterers of stealing their dog," she retorted.

"Uh. Well. How peculiar," Kate said. "It's this way," she gestured wildly, not looking at her visitor. "Just go up the stairs and straight ahead. This building is in the form of two flats now. I'm upstairs. But, anyway, what's all this about a stolen dog? What's it got to do with me?"

Ahead of her on the stairs Honoraria stopped and turned around. "Because it's Mr Wisley who's rung me. And it's you who's stolen his dog, of course!"

"Let's get upstairs and sit down," Kate said, dragging her feet while her thoughts raced around trying to get themselves sorted. And failing.

Seated with hot chocolate and a plate of biscuits Kate said, "I have not stolen anyone's dog. And if you're going to persist with this ridiculous claim you'd better have good reason rather than just the say-so of some crank caller you've had." Her heart felt decidedly jumpy, but so far at least she was pleased with her lying. Usually she was hopeless at it. She must be a late bloomer on the lying front.

On the other hand, she wasn't really lying. Zorro had stolen the dog, not her. She was just looking after it for him. And he'd told her she hadn't stolen the dog. So, she hadn't stolen the dog. No. She was beginning to feel on dodgy ground, though, and had a horrible feeling that any minute now her nerve would break, she'd fling herself on the floor and confess everything. Somehow she had to hold out and not do that. She didn't want to get Zorro in trouble.

"Listen, Ms Benning. This is serious. Mr Wisley is furious. He wants his dog back."

Far from the effect Honoraria was hoping to create, this stiffened Kate's resolve. There was no way Weasel-Face was getting Rover back. That poor dog had suffered enough.

32

"You're bringing the name of our charity in to disrepute behaving like this, Ms Benning. You will be struck off our register of fosterers."

"You have absolutely no proof of anything," Kate said. "Why are you so certain I'm in the wrong? You might not have known me for long, but you've never even met Weasel-Face, so why are you so sure this is down to me?"

"Weasel-Face?" Honoraria queried faintly.

"Uh. Mr Wisley, I mean. I did go there and I nearly came away with Rover but Mr Wisley demanded money. Two hundred pounds. Should I have given him the money?"

"No. Certainly not!" Honoraria was visibly outraged at the very idea.

"So, when did I steal Rover exactly?" Kate demanded.

"Well, I don't know all the details…"

"You know more about me than you do about him and yet you're happy to accuse me of stealing his dog." Kate tried to look all hurt and maligned.

"The dog is right there. He's the dog in the room. So far we've managed to avoid talking about him, but he's right there. In front of us."

"That's not Rover!"

Rover responded to his name by wriggling along the carpet until he could rest his head on Kate's foot. Occasionally his tail would thump encouragingly.

"Who's that then?" Kate's visitor demanded.

"That's Princess Leia," Kate said. "Obviously." It was just as well his coat was so thick. It covered up evidence of his contrary gender.

"Oh, please," Honoraria said. "That has to be Rover."

Kate rechecked. No, there was nothing showing. Rover's tail thumped rhythmically. Kate was sure he smiled.

"Of course it isn't. Rover is black and white and has no brown on him. I saw him quite clearly when I was there. No brown at all. Princess Leia obviously has lots of brown. Also, Rover wasn't wearing a balaclava. And he didn't look the type to wear one, either."

The dye had worked really quite well. Kate was pleased with it. And she'd managed to match up the dye with the wool for the balaclava, too. Rover made a great tricolour Border Collie now.

"I thought you didn't have a dog," Honoraria said suspiciously. "And that's why you wanted to foster – so you could sometimes have a dog but it wouldn't be totally your responsibility."

"That was the idea, but I was given this dog last night. After I'd tried to get Rover and failed. I was given this dog."

"You were given this dog?" Kate was amazed at how bland Honoraria managed to keep her voice.

"Yes, that's right."

"By whom?"

"Not that it's anything to do with you, but Princess Leia was given to me by my, er, my hero."

"Your hero? You mean, your fiancé?"

"Uh. Yes." What else could she say? She could hardly say Zorro had appeared as if by magic and rescued a dog in distress for her.

Honoraria sighed heavily. "I don't know what to say. Mr Wisley was most insistent."

"You can tell him you've seen me and you've seen my dog and it's not Rover. There's nothing else you *can* say."

"No. True. Actually, there *is* something else I need to say to you. And that is that, regretfully, I'm closing the charity. I only started it a short time ago and really, I had no idea of the multitude of details involved and I'm not coping with it properly. I'm going to have to call it a day. I think my money would be better spent in someone else's hands – still on behalf of dogs that need a home, of course."

"I'm sorry to hear that. There's obviously a lot of need." But, Kate thought, it actually worked quite well for her in covering up another bit of her criminal career. She felt badly for the dogs that wouldn't be saved though.

"Well, you've done your bit, taking in Princess Leia."

34

"I have thought since having her that if I was only fostering Princess Leia I would find it very difficult to let her go to anyone else now, and I've only had her a few hours."

"A lot of fosterers do stop being fosterers with their first dog for this very reason," Honoraria agreed. "Anyway, I'd better go."

As she rose to leave, the doorbell rang so Kate and her visitor simply continued on down the stairs to the front door, Kate switching on the lights as they went.

On the doorstep stood Weasel-Face.

"Hello Mr Wisley," Kate said. "This is a little late for calling isn't it?"

"I want the money. Or the dog."

"I don't have your dog. And the charity doesn't work like that."

"Give me the money! Or the dog." He had a mulish expression on his weaselly face. It didn't sit at all well on his features.

"Wait a minute. How do you know where I live?" Was he following her after all?

"Give me the money!" He demanded.

Kate was relieved that Honoraria hadn't immediately made off leaving her on her own with Weasel-Face, and even more grateful when she intervened on Kate's behalf, too.

"Mr Wisley," she said. "I'm Honoraria Jamieson. We spoke on the phone a little earlier. You're the reason I'm here. You're the reason I've been on a wild goose chase at three in the morning on New Year's Day. You're also the reason I'm about to call on the police station. You can't go round making wild accusations about people and expect to get away with it. Nor can you expect to turn up on people's doorsteps at ridiculous times in the night and demand money. You will get no money, and your dog is not here. If he ever was your dog in the first place, which I'm beginning to doubt. The only dog here is Princess Leia Organa of Alderaan."

With a gesture towards Rover, Honoraria – who apparently was a Star Wars fan under that sensible cardigan and cameo brooch ensemble – continued. "As you can see, this dog is a tricolour. Your dog is not. You said so yourself. So I'm forced to conclude that this is some sort of scam. I dread to think what you want other people's dogs for." She gave a visible shudder and stared at Weasel-Face as though he were the worst type of human detritus that had ever littered the earth.

Which maybe he was for all Kate knew. He certainly hadn't endeared himself to her earlier, but she felt sorry for him now. She wouldn't like to be on the end of that stare. It was downright scary!

It appeared he thought so too. He backed away, mumbling, "I'm sorry to have bothered you. This dog isn't Rover. I made a mistake and won't be accusing anyone of anything again." He shot Kate a murderous look, and made off into the darkness.

Kate's feelings of guilt multiplied exponentially, but she still knew she wasn't going to give Rover up to someone who so obviously didn't care about him. In fact, it was a puzzle as to why Weasel-Face would come out in the middle of the night to claim him. Or maybe it was just the money he was after. Well, he could have the money. Kate had it all ready. It would make her feel better about the whole thing too. More legal, somehow.

She glanced up at Honoraria and cringed. Somehow *she* was on the end of That Stare, now, and no matter how hard she tried, she couldn't pull her gaze away and had to wait for whatever fate was about to befall her. Rover, feeling her pain, crawled over to her and flopped on her feet as if to say that as long as her toes were warmed by him she'd be fine.

Finally, Honoraria spoke: "I strongly suggest you rinse this dog again before he gets any more of that caramel colour on your carpets, and I also strongly suggest you introduce him as Prince Leia rather than Princess if you wish to retain any credibility whatsoever. I won't see you again. Happy New Year." And she, too, disappeared into the night.

Looking down Kate saw that Rover now lay on his back grinning to himself and peddling his paws in the air inviting anyone who was willing to give him a belly rub. He had no modesty that dog! And no takers for the belly rub either.

Chapter Four

About to go back in, this time to bed, Kate stopped as a car pulled up. The driver must be coming to her place. There was nowhere else to go down here. Trying to peer through the night shadows her heart decided to stop for a moment and then to start up again in an uneven canter. Which was all very alarming.

All because it thought it saw Zorro getting out of the car.

Immobile, her breath coming in faster and faster gasps, she watched as the figure approached. Dizziness threatened to overtake her so it was lucky that Zorro stepped into the patch of light shining out of the hall window – and turned into Errol Hamilton, the youngest of the three Hamilton boys and the one she saw least of because he was a literary writer who lived in a warehouse and was generally anti-social as befitted a serious writer.

"Kate," he said before he'd reached her. "Where were you? We missed you tonight. It's the first time any member of The Three Families has escaped a New Year do since time began. I was told you were ill so I thought as I was passing, I'd check up on you. I saw your lights on. You okay?"

Having regained her breath, Kate mumbled: "I've got a stinking cold. That's why I didn't come. I'd have been terrible company."

She saw the theatrical way Errol flinched as Rover lumbered out to greet him.

"You've got a dog?" he said. "When did you get a dog?"

Kate knew as surely as she stood there that he was pretending to *not* know she had a dog. Why would he do that? Not only that, but it looked like Rover knew Errol even if Errol didn't know him. Kate had no clue why he'd behave so bizarrely so she decided to lie, too, to underline the fiction she'd decided upon. "I've had Princess Leia for about three weeks or so now," she said as casually as she could, her fingers crossed behind her back. Schooling her face to look like the sort of face anyone would trust, she stared in his direction.

"Princess Leia? As in Star Wars?" Errol asked.

"That's right. Princess Leia Organa of Alderaan to be absolutely correct."

"Isn't this sort of dog usually just black and white?"

"Quite often they have brown thrown in as well," Kate said. "Like Princess Leia."

And suddenly his interest in Rover switched off. Kate saw it, as though a shutter of indifference had come down. "I had no idea you had a dog," he said lamely.

She didn't know what to say to what she felt sure was a blatant lie, so she continued to stare at him, projecting her own I'm-not-lying face. It was all very mystifying. It would seem he'd called in at this hour of the night expecting to see Rover. How could he know anything about that at all? It also seemed that he lost interest as soon as he thought it wasn't Rover. What was so special about Rover? And what had Errol Hamilton got to do with anything?

"Goodness, Kate," Errol said. "You haven't looked at me like that since you had a crush on me when we were about thirteen."

"I had a crush on you?" She wasn't sure why she was so horrified at the idea. All The Three Families boys were capable of being heartthrob material and Errol was the closest in age to her of all of them. They had always got on well when younger and the older ones wanted them to clear off and leave them to their superior we're-older-than-you activities. But she had never thought of him in a romantic light. He had been too brother-like to ever consider him as anything else. She had never had a crush on him. Why would he make that up? Especially as they'd grown apart in their later teens and didn't have much to do with each other now.

Errol clutched his heart. "You don't remember? Oh, no. I am devastated, simply distraught."

He was going from bad to worse.

"Are you drunk?" she demanded. "If you are, you shouldn't be driving."

By this time Rover had got close enough to Errol to press himself up against his legs leaving an affectionate swathe of dog hairs across the black fabric of his trousers. "I'm not drunk. I'll be sending you the dry cleaning bill for these trousers," he said, backing away from Rover who thought it was a game and followed. But Errol wasn't interested and sprinted back to his car. "I'll see you tomorrow at the New Year's Day dinner," he shouted. "You look recovered enough to attend. Do you think you'll be there?"

"Yes," she shouted back.

Kate had thought she might give that meal a miss as well, but the hassle associated with non-attendance of both traditional Three Families New Year shindigs was probably greater than the hassle of going, even though she really didn't feel well at all. The excitement of rescuing Rover had kept it at bay for a while but it was making itself felt again now.

On top of which, the events of the night were all very puzzling. Her flat wasn't on the way to anywhere and yet Errol had said he was just passing. Mulling it over, she squirmed as she remembered the crush that he'd referred to. She'd actually had an enormous crush on Tom Cole, not Errol Hamilton, but at eighteen he wasn't interested in the thirteen year old girl he'd grown up with, and so, in a vain attempt to make Tom jealous, she'd pretended that she actually lusted after Errol. Kate came over all hot and cold thinking about it now. How embarrassing to remember that! How awful it must have been at the time.

He couldn't possibly be Zorro, could he? Errol Hamilton, writer of stuff she didn't understand; semi-hermit in his warehouse; a bit of a Lothario by all accounts, or at least by Bridget's accounts. Bridget had always had her eye on Errol before she became engaged to the middle Hamilton brother, Spencer, Tom's best friend and partner in their accountancy firm. Well, when she wasn't lusting after Clark, the eldest Hamilton boy, that was…

When she and Spencer seriously got together Bridget had to get all respectable. You can't get engaged to an accountant and turn up at his company dinners in leathers and studs and black make up, not if you then wanted to marry him… And Bridget did want to marry Spencer. He was her meal ticket, her way forward to a pampered and idle existence. She was perfectly open about it. She didn't ever want to have to work. An accountant hubby was ideal, as long as he had some ambition, of course. Bridget would make sure Spencer did have some ambition. Poor Spencer.

Anyway, Kate had been up quite long enough, especially for someone with a stinking cold. The fireworks seemed to have finally petered out so she didn't need to switch on the various noise-disguising appliances again, thankfully. Just as well she had no immediate neighbours or she wouldn't be able to use that strategy to drown out the dog-terrorising noises.

She made for bed, followed by Rover who had no doubt in his heart at all, that wherever Kate laid her head, so would he. His confidence was not misplaced although she drew the line at him actually on the bed. He had to be content with the floor, but close enough to Kate so that in the night when she stretched out her fingers she could feel his fur and hear his nearly-snore.

Chapter Five

The front door slammed, jerking Kate from sleep and alerting her to Bridget's arrival in the house. Rover jumped on her bed as if that was the correct response to someone's appearance in the building. Absently, Kate patted him. She was thinking that it was time to get her key back from Bridget. Now she had Rover in residence she couldn't have anyone walking into her home without any warning, in case they let him out. Hopefully Bridget wouldn't get too offended, although she could get offended all by herself these days. It was a shame, but their friendship did seem to be wearing a bit thin.

Kate listened to Bridget's progress up the stairs, which meant she wasn't going into her own flat. She was coming up to Kate's. When she was about half way up a stray firework could clearly be heard outside. Rover leapt to his feet, launched himself off the bed, raced to the door, screamed at it, and, tail between his legs, tore across the bedroom towards her and leapt back on the bed. It was as if he didn't know what to do with himself.

"You don't have to worry!" Kate put her arms around him. She hugged him hard and murmured into his fur, but he was oblivious to her, so caught up was he in his own terror.

He continued with the strange, unearthly noise, quivering and staring at the doorway as though the thing making him afraid would shortly appear in the room. Kate assumed this behaviour was a result of his previous life of being horribly lonely punctuated by periods of utter dread when fireworks went off and the only thing slightly more tolerable was when someone turned up with a bucket of food.

However, she couldn't let him keep on like this. It surely wasn't good for him, not to mention her nightie was fast being shredded by his scrabbling claws as he tried to climb up it to yell right into her face. She wound her arms around him and gripped him hard.

When Bridget appeared, she did so very slowly, easing herself into the room and watching Rover with great apprehension. Kate couldn't blame her. Rover was making the kind of noise you'd expect to hear on a deserted moor watched over by a blood-spattered moon.

"Just ignore him," Kate yelled. "Just ignore him and he'll be quiet in a minute. Just sit down and wait it out."

It took a surprisingly short time before the racket petered out and Rover lay on the floor panting, a somewhat dazed look in his eyes. Kate was pleased she'd spent some time checking on the internet about dog-whispering and how wolves behave in packs. She'd have to learn more about it.

"What is that?" Bridget said, her eyes round as she stared at Rover as if he were a bucket of slugs.

"He is a poor, rescued dog," Kate said. "He's been left on his own over firework season. It's no wonder he's in a state." She couldn't believe how defensive she felt. She barely knew Rover, but it was like she was standing up for her own kin.

"No, I mean – what is *that*?" Bridget pointed at Rover's head.

"That's his firework balaclava. Good idea, if I do say so myself, although I've since found others so it's not an original idea. The extra thickness over his ears hopefully muffles some of the frightening noises."

"He looks ridiculous. That's probably the real reason he was screaming. He was proclaiming his outrage at being made to wear something that makes him look like Princess Leia."

"It doesn't matter what he looks like as long as it works. You don't look too great yourself. Do I gather you were up all night at The Three Families party?"

"Of course I was. It's traditional. You should have been there."

"I was ill."

"Not too ill to go and rescue a dog, it would seem. Just too ill to be nice to Tom. Tom – your fiancé – my brother. Remember him? Not to mention too ill to come to the party that we've all been to every year for the whole of our lives. It's not good enough, Kate. It's not just about you, you know. All the parents were disappointed you weren't there, and Tom was devastated. You owe it to all of us to do your bit."

"I know he's your brother and all, but I owe him nothing. I don't owe anyone anything. Especially when I'm so ill. I went to bed early on New Year's Eve, that's how ill I was." Well, she had meant to. She had felt ill enough to do that.

"You still went out and got a dog," Bridget persisted. "You can't have been that ill."

"Hang on a minute. How do you know I went out and rescued a dog last night?"

"You told me," Bridget declared.

"I did not."

"You told me you were going to be a dog fosterer and today you have a dog."

Kate was letting her imagination get away with her, spooking at shadows, seeing heroes, seeing villains. It must be the cold making her feverish.

"Sorry," Kate said. "You're right. I did tell you that. However, this isn't that dog. This is another dog. That dog wasn't a tricolour." Carrying swiftly on, Kate said: "You know, there is a difference between being so ill you haven't got what it takes to be sociable just because you always have, and being so ill you can still do something you think is the right thing because someone else is worse off." As she said it she knew she was muddling herself with her lies. Maybe it would be better if she tried to avoid the subject. Not least because Bridget knew very well she didn't have a dog yesterday.

But Bridget wasn't going to let it drop. "It's a dog!"

"And your point is?"

"My point is that it's a *dog*!"

Kate tried to hang on to her temper. "Yes, Bridget. He is indeed a dog. An innocent and defenceless creature in need of help because of the so-called superior species – that's us, by the way. Existing in fear and horrible loneliness due to uncaring humans. He needed a hand. I chose to give it to him. It's not for you to judge me and I don't understand why you're being so naff about it. But I tell you what. For once, I'm not going to do the docile thing and roll over and die. Get used to it!"

Bridget stared at her as though she was a soft, fluffy toy who had got up and viciously attacked her leg. Which just went to show, as far as Kate was concerned, that she'd spent way too much of her life doing what was expected of her instead of doing what she wanted. Well, the soft, fluffy worm had turned now.

And it was all thanks to Zorro and a dog in a Princess Leia balaclava who needed her. Somehow Zorro had given her courage when he'd stolen Rover for her. She felt a rush of gratitude. He was her hero indeed!

Bridget threw herself on the sofa and burst into tears. All her life Kate had dropped everything and rushed to her friend's aid, but this time she was holding a shivering dog, and she wasn't about to desert him for someone who obviously cared nothing for his well-being.

"But I needed you there…" Bridget wailed, heaving and sobbing and clutching her hair.

Kate was unmoved. She had seen it all before.

"Me and Spencer broke up! And Clark wasn't even there. And you weren't there, either."

"Even though you broke up with Spencer you still stayed all night?"

45

"Well, I wasn't going to leave before him, was I? Why should I? I have more right to be there than him anyway. You're my best friend. He's only a friend. And the party was at *your* parents' house this year, as well."

Kate despaired of ever being able to follow Bridget's reasoning. Things that quite often Bridget saw as being completely black and white, Kate didn't get at all. She always felt as though she was missing something when she didn't see it the way Bridget did.

"Come here," Kate ordered. Rover still cowered under one of her arms so Bridget scooted across the floor, climbed on the bed and pulled the other around her shoulders and sobbed brokenly.

Kate leaned back against the headboard and considered the last twelve hours. She'd managed to annoy The Three Families by not turning up for their time-honoured New Year's Eve bash; she was harbouring a stolen dog that looked like Princess Leia; she was experiencing unfamiliar feelings of impatience with her best friend which she knew would previously have filled her with despair; and she still had a stinking cold, although it had receded somewhat.

But also, she had met Zorro – her man of mystery, her hero, her undercover knight in a balaclava. Firmly, she banished him from her immediate thoughts. She'd save him for later.

In the meantime, she would have to make an effort to appear for the New Year's Day Dinner. The Three Families always collected together for this in the same house as the New Year's Eve bash so that there was really only one lot of mess to clear up, and whoever was due to host these events had three years in which to plan for them, and the other two families just had to turn up and enjoy themselves.

But she wasn't about to go out and leave Rover on his own yet. He didn't know his new home well enough to leave him alone in it, and it was still firework season. He'd just have to come too. Kate could wear a black waistcoat and go as Hans Solo and with her dog they'd be Star Wars characters and could pretend they thought it was a fancy dress year. She nearly laughed aloud but realised in time that Bridget was still in dramatic-mode so she stifled her mirth.

"Bridge – why did you break up with Spencer?" Kate knew it wouldn't have come from Spencer. He loved Bridget with an intensity and focus that Bridget revelled in, but that Kate found faintly repulsive.

"He's decided the wedding should wait for a couple of years until he's more sure of the business, given the *'parlous state of the economy'*," Bridget mimicked in a sing-song voice nothing like Spencer's growly tones.

"But he still wants to marry you," Kate stated, knowing full well that would be the case.

"Of course he does! But I want it to be sooner rather than later. I don't want to have to keep waiting."

"What difference does it make? You spend all your time at his house anyway. You already do everything together. You go on a million holidays together so it can't be the honeymoon you're yearning for. The wedding is really only a big party for all of us isn't it?"

Bridget jerked upright, Kate's arm falling away from her. Outrage sharpened her tone. Kate knew what was coming and resigned herself to the inevitable ticking off. "You have no soul, Kate! You have no romance in your soul. I want to be Mrs Spencer Hamilton. I want it to be official. I want every other woman in the world to know he's mine."

Kate tried to keep her face expressionless.

"Oh, I know you don't like all that possessiveness and stuff, but normal people do, Kate. If you were normal, you'd have married poor old Tom by now instead of breaking up with him. You're both of you all lost and alone now. It's only natural that I want to tie Spencer down and he wants to tie me down, too. Or he should. It's just being an accountant has made him more cautious than he needs to be. That's what it is. As if the *'parlous state of the economy'* is going to affect us!"

They'd been through all this before. Kate was not about to try and justify herself again. "And what was that you said about Clark not being there?" she queried hoping to change the subject. "Is he reporting from some hot spot somewhere in the world? A war zone or something?"

Bridget pulled a face. "Yeah. What was that about? Actually he did turn up this morning, but really only in time for breakfast. I don't think he'd just flown in from somewhere, although he didn't say. The point is, he wasn't there when I needed him when Spencer got so horrible with me."

"Are you and Clark still...?"

"No! Of course not. That was ages ago, and it was only a bit of hanky-panky. But he should still have been there for the whole party, especially when I needed him. As you should have been, too." Bridget stopped and Kate imagined the cogs whirring under all that praline and caramel-coloured hair. She just managed to stop herself from checking Rover's legs to see if they really were the same colour.

"Hang on a minute," Bridget said, her mouth tightening. "It's all a bit of a coincidence isn't it? You and Clark not at the party for the first time in its history. You weren't having a clandestine meet up were you?"

"Don't be daft. I was ill. Remember? Anyway, I can't even think when I saw him last. What with him constantly going off abroad, and whatever else it is he does." For a moment she wondered if he might be Zorro, but only for a moment. "Tom wasn't there for a big chunk of the evening either. So maybe it's Clark and Tom who were having a clandestine meet up. Although I don't think so as Tom was here spying on me."

But Bridget had lost interest. "You *will* be there tonight, won't you? I made Clark promise he would be, and of course Tom will be there. You have no excuse. Even if your cold was very bad last night it doesn't seem too bad now."

"You're right. It does seem a bit better. I'll be there as long as I can take Princess Leia. I'm not leaving him here on his own. There'll be fireworks going off. I'll ring Dad in a bit and check with the parents about taking Princess Leia along. I'm a bit worried, though, because I don't know what he's like with a lot of people around. I don't know him very well yet."

"He's a dog, Kate. You don't need to know him very well. He should just do what he's told."

Kate stared at Bridget and wondered how well she'd ever known *her*. Bridget was her best friend! They'd lived next door to each other all through childhood, and now they even shared the same building, although thankfully in separate bits of it because the house behind the florist shop had been split into flats.

They had joined forces to rent this property when the old nurseryman retired. Bridget loved dealing with the public and Kate didn't, so it worked out well when they divided the business and Bridget ran the florist shop out the front, while Kate started to build her fuchsia specialist business in the nursery behind it. She loved growing things and was becoming quite well known in the fuchsia world, whereas she'd realised only recently that all along Bridget had just been marking time, playing at floristry until she got married. It also meant they spent little time together now, which suited Kate well.

In a small effort to atone for the guilt that thought produced, she said, "I'll drive us to the dinner. Okay? Then you can drink."

It also meant they'd be going in her car which had enough space for Rover in the boot. She thought she shouldn't be drunk in charge of a dog anyway.

"No, it's all right, thanks. I made Clark promise he'd be there, but I told him an earlier time than your mum said, so I can make up to him before Spencer gets there and then that'll put Spencer's nose out of joint. Serve him right. If I drink too much I'll stay over-night. Your mum always puts us up. You could do that, too."

"I probably won't. I'll want to get Princess Leia home."

Bridget snorted – a telling, if explosive, summary of what she thought of Kate's preoccupation with her furry friend. "Right, I'm off," she said. "All my gear for tonight is at home. I had to get Mum to shorten and iron the dress. See you later." And she was gone.

Kate tried to imagine asking her own mother, the formidable Stella Benning, to do some sewing and ironing for her and laughed aloud at the outrage she knew that request would produce! Not that she'd dare ask in the first place...

Chapter Six

A guilty conscience prevented Kate from making up for lost sleep. Thought of her mother made Kate feel guilty. It always did. This time, though, she'd brought the guilt on herself. She'd stolen a dog! She also felt guilty about not going to the New Year's Eve bash but at least she knew she really had been too ill to socialise. Then there was her break up with Tom. She still felt guilty about that although she wasn't sure why she should. She just did. It made her feel mean.

She couldn't do anything about any of it except maybe the theft of the dog, and she had to do something about that or she'd always be on edge, afraid that someone would have the right to take Rover off her and subject him to loneliness and fireworks again.

If she handed over the money Weasel-Face wanted then surely that meant Rover was definitely hers and he couldn't be taken from her. She was a bit hazy about the legalities but it made sense to her, and there was no one she could trust enough to ask for confirmation.

It would be a relief to start the New Year with a clear conscience. She gave up trying to get any sleep and counted the two hundred pounds she'd drawn out earlier. Not finding an envelope, she shoved it into a poo bag. She had loads of poo bags all ready for when a dog bounced into her life. She tied the handles of the bag into a firm knot so the dosh couldn't fall out, and headed off into the very early morning, her trusty dog at her side. Rover hopped into the boot of the car as though he'd been doing it all his life. No arguments this time about his belief that he belonged in the front passenger seat.

Kate took the road back to Rover's House of Hell. Fleetingly, the thought crossed her mind that Zorro might be there, but just as fleetingly she squashed the idea. She was only going to right a wrong. That was all. She wanted to make it so that no one had any grounds to come and take Rover away from her. She definitely wasn't going back just in case she saw Zorro again.

But if she did see him again, she wouldn't close her eyes. No, indeedy – she would take a good look at the bonus she'd been thrown.

Driving up the street to where Zorro might be waiting and Weasel-Face hopefully not, Kate found the turn into that road had been blocked off. She pulled to a halt just past what would have been the turn-off. Damn. She'd have to walk now. She had wanted to simply drive by the house, throw the money at Weasel-Face and speed off. At least it was cool enough to leave Rover in the car without worrying about him asphyxiating in the two minutes she expected to be away from it.

But maybe it was too cool. Maybe he'd freeze to death instead. She hadn't realised what a worry having a dog in her life would be.

Rover, as if sensing her anxiety rested the full weight of his head on her arm and it gave her strength. She hugged him and left him, locking the car as she went.

A bystander leaning against the wall waved his thumb in the direction of the barricades. "You won't get up there. All those streets are cordoned off. Big drug raid, love. In the night. We've been told we have to detour around. They even had the helicopter out. All night. Thundering away there. Think all the Counters got away, though. Let's face it, they usually do."

"Really? They usually get away?" Kate had no idea what he was talking about – counters? – but she tried to look interested.

"Yeah. I opened my own front door to see what all the racket was about and an armed police officer told me to get back inside. Bloody nerve. My own front door. There were traffic officers, armed police officers, sniffer dogs everywhere, choppers, the lot."

Wow. This really was the Badlands. They probably had this kind of kerfuffle every night. "I just want to call on a house round the corner. Surely I can do that," Kate said with a sinking feeling that she already knew what he was going to say.

"Nah. No one in or out unless you're one of them." He gestured with his thumb at a couple of people wearing white protective suits, and a policeman with a dog. "One of those dogs found bags of Bennies stashed inside the door frames. Actually in the door frame! Who'd ever think of that!"

"Bennies?"

"Yeah. You know. Copilots. Crank. Dexies." He looked at her. "Speed."

"Ah. Speed. I've heard of speed." Kate had heard of speed. She didn't know what it was, but she had heard of it.

"It's an organisation, you know. The Counters. Someone is dealing to them and they're dealing to dealers on the street."

"Uh. Yeah." Kate couldn't decide what to do. She smiled her thanks at the guy with the gesturing thumb who knew a great deal more about how all this worked than she did, or than she ever wanted to know, and turned back to the car. As she was about to unlock her door, she glanced over the car roof and spotted Zorro.

He was running down the other side of the street. As she watched, he abruptly dived behind a hedge. He could have been anyone wearing black jeans, black top and a black balaclava. Anyone. Except that when his eyes rested momentarily on Kate, her heart tried to leap out of her chest because it wanted to join his, and she knew that he couldn't possibly be just anyone – he had to be her Zorro. Even if he turned out to be a drug baron running away, which is what it looked like in this particular setting at this particular moment, he was still her Zorro.

In that moment she knew she was a goner. She knew she was hooked. To think she'd thought she was in love with Tom for all those years. Now she really knew what 'being in love' meant, and she could do nothing about it.

She watched the hedge but Zorro didn't reappear. If he *was* a drug dealer then her love was doomed. She was destined to be single for her entire life and just live amongst her fuchsias. With her trusty dog at her feet.

"Well, look who it is," a voice announced. "It's that Kate Benning, one of the exalted Three Families. See, I found out who you are. That's how I knew where you lived. Oh, and look, that's nice, you've brought Princess Leia Organa of Alderaan with you, the dog who is definitely not Rover." Weasel-Face loomed over her.

Kate flinched. Where had he come from so suddenly? Still, he was the reason she was here.

"I was looking for you," she said. "Here you are!" She shoved the poo bag at him. Involuntarily his hand came out and he took it.

"What is it?" he demanded, eyeing it with a look of revulsion. Not that it altered his Weasel-Face much.

"It's the money you wanted. Now you have no rights over him because I've bought him for the money you demanded. So it's a done deal. Agreed?"

Weasel-Face opened his mouth but whatever he might have been about to say went unuttered because a shout went up further down the street. Kate glanced in that direction and looked back in time to see Weasel-Face disappearing down the same way Zorro had gone.

She wondered if she'd just given two hundred quid to a drug dealer. She hoped if she had that he'd get shot of the dosh before it came into police hands and they got her fingerprints off it. Good grief. Could she get any more involved with a criminal undertaking if she tried harder?

Kate opened the boot lid and put her arms around Rover's neck, burying her face in his biscuity-smelling fur.

"You'd better hope that dosh doesn't get traced back to me or you'll lose your new home before you're properly in it," she mumbled. He licked her ear in reassurance. He was sure she'd be okay. She was innocent. All she'd done was buy a dog, after all. When looked at in a certain light.

A dreadful unease overtook her and the suspicion that the drug raid had been on Rover's former home became a certainty. And her DNA and bits of skin and fallen-out hair and God knows what else would be all over the place. She gave Rover an extra hard hug and decided she'd better get out of here as soon as possible. Stepping back she checked none of Rover's extremities were in danger of being pruned by the boot lid, and slammed it shut.

Straightening up she flinched as a hand came down on her shoulder and a feeling of déjà vu enveloped her. She turned, her instant excited anticipation of seeing Zorro dashed when she caught sight of Clark Hamilton. Still, it was nice to see Clark.

"What are you doing here? How lovely to see you. It's been so long," she said, balancing on tiptoe to plant a kiss on his cheek. He'd always been more like a brother to her than her own brother. "I heard from Bridget that you missed the party last night. You bad lad. I did too, so I'm in disgrace as well."

"Yep. We're both in the dog house all right. There's no one I'd rather share a kennel with than you, however."

"Always the charmer," Kate said absently. She was trying to keep an eye out for Zorro so she wasn't really concentrating on Clark, but the tone of his voice made her look more carefully at him when he said, "Talking of dog-things. What have you done to this poor creature? He must be blushing under his fur with that thing on his head." He pointed at Rover who was trying to lick his way through the back window of the car, his tail thrashing about so fast Kate couldn't figure out why his rear end didn't take flight.

"No, he's not blushing. It's a special balaclava to keep the noise of fireworks and thunder out so he's not so frightened of them." *And he's in disguise, too, of course, but I can't tell you that.* "Will you be at the dinner tonight?" she asked, to divert him from the subject of doggy balaclava fashion.

"Oh, yes. Try and keep me away," he said. "Going to have to make up for lost ground with the parents you know, having not been there last night."

She eyed him curiously. "That's never bothered you before," she said. "You've always gone your own way."

"There is no other way to go, is there?"

"Well..." She knew there was, and she was beginning to realise that she'd always taken all the other ways apart from her own. But now, having Zorro in her life was showing her that she had always tried to please everyone else first and herself last.

Apart from the fuchsias.

No one had seen that coming. Not even her. It was a shame in a way that her growing reputation in the fuchsia world made it more acceptable to her family and friends than when she first started out. She missed the feeling that she was blazing a trail for herself without their permission. It was probably the first time in her life that she'd struck out on her own against everyone's wishes and it had felt good. Scary, but good.

Maybe it was time to do it again. And falling in love so suddenly with Zorro was the perfect reason to try. Unless he turned out to be a drug dealer in which case she really couldn't justify it. She had to draw the line somewhere.

"So," she said. "What are you doing here?"

"I'm doing a series of related articles on the drug scene in the South West and police attempts at clearing it up. That's why I'm here. I got word of the raid." He gestured over his shoulder.

"Goodness. I hope you're not getting into any dangerous situations!"

"No, of course not! I'm standing well back here." He grinned at her and Kate realised that she didn't really know what he'd been up to over the last couple of years. She also realised what a charming grin he had. Her stomach flipped.

Was Clark her Zorro? She stared at him. Oh, God. Was he Zorro? He was the oldest of The Three Families children and she was the youngest. The gap in age had always seemed so enormous as children. But now... Well, now... not so much... He was seven years older than her, which was nothing now.

The thought that he might be her new love, without her realising it, so threw her that to cover her confusion she turned away and made a production of opening the boot lid to let Rover out. The dog was practically turning himself inside out in his excitement to get to a new human. Rover fell on Clark as though he was a long lost friend. There followed a bout of playful wrestling which left Clark, who was clad all in black, Kate now realised, covered in dog hair.

Then as suddenly as he'd appeared he was gone with a wave and a "See you tonight," lingering in her ears. Kate and Rover got back in the car, and left the scene of her crime, which is what it could be if she had indeed just handed money over to a drug baron.

And if the raid had been on Rover's House of Hell, now carpeted in her DNA, maybe sirens would start screaming, and law enforcement types swarm all over her and her dog. She wanted to put her foot down and zoom off, but she forced herself to drive well within the speed limit so no one would think she was running away from anything.

But whether she wanted to run from the scene of a drug deal with her grubby two hundred quid implicating her, or the scene of her infatuation with Zorro, she wasn't sure.

Chapter Seven

Kate dragged herself up the stairs after Rover who bounded up them as though he'd been doing it all his life. She was so tired! Her cold, although better, was still a drain on her energies. To be fair, she had been up all night rescuing dogs, tackling criminals, meeting her hero, falling in love, not to mention disguising a dog. It was hardly surprising that she was exhausted.

She had to go to the dinner tonight, whether she wanted to or not. She felt shattered, but not nearly as decrepit as she'd felt last night, and she would be really dicing with death if she swerved The Three Families New Year's Day dinner as well.

Not only that, but she didn't want to let Tom down more than she already had. Since she broke up with him in September, she'd been careful to appear when he needed to look like he was one of an engaged couple. She was beginning to tire of the need, but if it helped him get over it – her carrying on the masquerade, then she would. It had been the only thing he had asked of her after his initial shock and devastation at her breaking it off. So she still had to wear the ring, of course, but that was okay.

It worried her that he still fostered hopes of them getting back together. She was going to have to have words with him – again – and be more firm about it, although she had some difficulty seeing how she could be any clearer than, "I don't want to marry you, Tom." But she would have to try.

Having decided she was definitely going to the dinner, she collapsed in a heap on the sofa and was instantly asleep.

She woke up very gradually and lay still waiting for full consciousness to return. It was taking its time. Kate felt very hot and wondered whether she really was well enough to go out this evening. She tried to stretch a bit but found she couldn't. She was anchored in place by an unnatural heaviness. Oh, no, the bug must have really gone to town on her and reduced her to mewling weakness. Panic had her kicking against her sudden infirmity and she jerked upright, releasing herself from her temporary paralysis as Rover fell off her and off the sofa onto the floor with a piteous yelp.

Rover!

Kate leapt onto the floor with him and gave him a hug. Fancy forgetting she had a dog now. "Mind you," she said to him. "I didn't say anything about you being a furniture dog. You're not allowed on the furniture in future. Okay."

He stared at her so hard she could almost hear the cogs whirring in his brain as he tried to work out what she was saying.

She kissed his nose and straightened his balaclava which had come somewhat adrift in his slumbers with the result that one of Princess Leia's buns rested over his left eye, and the other sat on top of his head like a large cherry on a cup cake. Grateful that she'd restored his enchanting look he flicked her nose with his tongue. Then he stood by the door in that age-old posture that demanded a quick trot around the garden for relief purposes.

She snatched up some poo bags, grabbed Rover's leash, clipped it on, and they galloped down the stairs and outside. Kate was startled to see how dark it was. She hadn't realised she'd been asleep that long. Shadowy clouds drooped low in the heavens adding to the gloom of early evening that was the norm at this time of year. She wasn't late for The Three Families dinner yet…

59

Rover showed his gratitude to the great outdoors almost immediately, and Kate realised that, if there was one thing she wasn't going to like much about having a dog, it was going to be clearing up after him. Although, she supposed, that would be true of anything. If you kept lizards there would be something to clean up – actually, it would be a lot more because they changed their skin regularly. Aargh! Same for if you kept children or had a husband – although they should be able to clear up after themselves, she'd have thought. Unless they were Bridget.

Oh, well. It was a small price to pay for all that furry affection and loyalty. She scooped up Rover's offerings with her little black bag and stopped breathing while she tied knots in the top to prevent any escape. She hoped she would become more blasé about doing it, too, and stop caring if there was anyone else about or not. She carried on walking as casually as she could.

But there were other things to worry about as well – what about picking up poo in a high wind, with the flimsy poo bag blowing around all over the place? She was glad she had thought of it before there was a high wind – in future she would be sure to loosen the bags before even leaving the house so she wouldn't have to spend too long merely trying to get the thing open while a tornado ran her down.

She pictured herself standing over a steaming pile of poo wrestling with a recalcitrant poo bag that wouldn't open and having Zorro turn up at that point. Yes, she'd have to learn to be the speediest poo-picker-upper in the South West.

Zorro! Reflexively, she glanced over her shoulder. While she and Rover searched every shadow behind her, someone ran on soundless feet towards her and suddenly the poo bag was snatched from her hand. Swivelling back to see who it was, she could make out nothing of use in the gloom, only a shadow darker than those around it, running swiftly away.

The unexpectedness of the robbery made her heart leap about in her chest and she dropped Rover's lead. Luckily, he merely stared up at her, probably wondering why she'd dropped it. He was probably wondering why she bothered attaching it to him in the first place if all she did was drop it. He was obviously a very smart dog.

The figure that had run away from her was now entirely indistinguishable from the long shadows of evening. Kate couldn't even say if it had been male or female. It was worrisome that someone felt they could just run up to her, snatch her bag and run away.

At the same time, it saved her carrying a bag of poo around with her until she could find a decent way of dumping it. As it were.

Why would someone want her bag of poo? They can't have realised what it was in that bag, but what on earth did they think she would be carrying around in a little black plastic bag? Momentarily, an image came to mind of her putting the two hundred pounds guilt-money for Rover into a poo bag. Yes, there was that. But no-one saw that so how would anyone know to snatch a poo bag off her at every opportunity on the off chance that it contained a load of dosh? It made no sense. Her heart had settled back down to its usual beat again. It wasn't as if she could do anything about it. She couldn't even tell anyone about it.

She could just imagine how *that* would go…

Her: "Someone snatched my bag while I was walking Rover."

Bridget: "OMG! You must report it."

Kate: "But it was my poo bag."

Bridget: "Your poo bag? What poo bag? What's a poo bag?"

Kate: "It's a bag for dog poo."

Bridget: "Why would you want a bag for dog poo?"

Kate: "So as to pick it up and not leave it lying around. Like you'd pick up any rubbish you dropped."

Bridget: "Oh. Well. You don't seem to have one."

Kate: "That's the point. I no longer have a poo bag because it was snatched."

Bridget: "Why would anyone want your poo bag?"

Kate: "I have no idea."

Bridget: "Maybe *they* needed one."

Kate: "This one was already full."

Bridget: "Ewww... Well, there's no point reporting a poo bag being pinched, is there, especially a used one. What a stupid idea!"

Kate: "Er... Quite so."

Bridget: "What a stupid conversation this is."

Kate: "Um. Yeah."

Nah. She wasn't about to tell anyone at all. No one. Not one person.

And then he was there. One minute, no one. The next, a figure materialised out of the darkness in front of her. Her heart didn't just slam into her chest wall this time. It did a treble flip first and then thundered so loud she couldn't hear anything but its beating in her head. It was Zorro!

"Ahhh," she managed, clutching tightly onto Rover's leash as he jumped up and down greeting the dark figure standing before them.

"Er, hello," Kate ventured, trying for a cool tone. Rover wagged his tail energetically and Kate knew without looking that he'd have a grin on his face. He loved everyone, that dog.

"Hello," Zorro whispered.

Kate had been hoping for a proper voice this time. They weren't so close to other people here. He could afford to talk more loudly. And if he did, she'd hope to get a clue as to who he might be. But, no, he whispered, obviously wanting to keep her mystified for longer. Well. She could cope with that. In the back of her mind was the idea that once his real identity was discovered, her Zorro might turn out to be just another normal, disappointing man. She already knew enough of them. For as long as he was a mystery she could dream; when the mystery was solved she couldn't.

"Hello," she whispered back. "I wondered where you were." Then she blushed fiercely, glad of the cover the night gave her. She hadn't meant to make it so obvious that she'd been thinking of him.

62

"I'm always there when you need someone," he whispered back.

"Well, he got away, so you were a little late," she couldn't help but point this out, romantic figure or no. She'd got to the stage of not really looking at him, afraid she might throw herself into his arms to be whisked away on horseback to a life of romance and passion. Also, if she really looked at him he might simply disappear. Maybe he was just a figment of her overheated and feverish imagination. She still wasn't brilliantly well.

Also, she wasn't really that keen on horses...

"Did he hurt you?"

Was that also her imagination, or was there fear for her in his voice? She smiled a little smile to herself. This romantic mystery was going very well. "No. But he did get away with my... er... my bag."

"I'm so glad you are unhurt. I would never have forgiven myself if you'd been harmed because I arrived too late. But your bag? I must get it back for you. Tell me what it looks like."

Rats! Whatever possessed her to mention it? Especially after deciding she never would. Now what was she going to say?

This time she stared up at him as though doing so might drive the thought of the bag from his mind and she wouldn't have to confess it was black polythene filled with stuff Rover no longer wanted. "Uh..."

Casting about for some reasonable way of making him forget the bag, she noticed that his shirt cuff was sticking out in the gap between the end of his black sleeve and where his black glove had rolled down. The material glowed in the moonlight like white does under strobe lights in a night club. He was wearing cufflinks. They were in the shape of a Jaguar. Kate had given Tom Jaguar-shaped cufflinks a few years ago as a birthday present. She knew he admired the animals but also it was a pun on his car.

What on earth was Zorro doing with Tom's cufflinks? Horror made her stare at him even harder. Was she wrong?

63

Was her Zorro a baddie after all, a burglar who'd been around the empty houses stealing all the jewellery, knowing everyone was celebrating the New Year elsewhere? Why would a burglar put on something he'd just stolen that night? How would he know who wouldn't be at home, although every local would know it was The Three Families tradition to be in one of their houses.

It was possible that Tom and Zorro had the same cufflinks, but somehow it seemed unlikely.

She would have noticed if her original Zorro at Rover's House of Hell had even been wearing any cufflinks, especially when she'd fallen back on him like she had when Rover jumped on her. He not only hadn't been wearing cufflinks – he hadn't been wearing a shirt with cuffs. His top and his gloves had been way too tight-fitting to get cuffs in there. She had actually noticed this. She blushed, remembering. This wasn't *her* Zorro standing before her now! This was someone else entirely!

While she was staring at his shirt the impostor-probably-a-burglar-Zorro was looking all around him as if he expected the poo bag thief to reappear. Kate tried to work out his height thinking that if she could make a note of such things she could at least compare them with the next time she did see Zorro, or a Zorro lookalike, but it was difficult to tell in the gloom whether he was standing on exactly the same level as she was or not. It wasn't a very level road they were on. But if he *was* on the same level, then he could be any one of The Three Families younger generation of males. Or it needn't have anything to do with any of them.

Although wearing all black clothes and a black balaclava might not be that uncommon, it seemed odd to think there might be more than one Zorro. How many more might appear to her offering help? It was a bit suspicious and the feeling in Kate's stomach of vast disappointment made her wonder if she'd been building up something that didn't exist. All from the stranger in the mask she'd initially seen when she went to rescue Rover.

How could she do that to herself? Life was just a series of disappointments, some big, mostly small, and she only added to them herself whenever she allowed her imagination to run away with her, especially regarding a romantic interest in her life.

All her life, fuelled by a shared childhood and the expectations of others, she had imagined a love affair with Tom which would last until they were buried together with clasped hands in the same grave, having died at the same time. And look how that ended! Not even with an explosion, but merely with a whimper. Nevertheless, it was her own fault that she'd imagined it into something else, something more romantic than it could ever possibly be.

She knew those cufflinks really well. She'd seen them often enough. And she recognised the chip out of the corner of the one he always wore in his left cuff. Tom was like that. He would always wear the one with the chip in his left cuff because he was right-handed and so he would assume fewer people would see the left cuff than the right. If these were the other way around then she would know for certain that it was someone pretending to be Tom pretending to be Zorro.

But they weren't the other way around. They were the right way around. She tried to contain her anger.

"Tom," she said, softly but distinctly. "What are you doing?"

"Pardon?" he whispered. "What did you say?"

"Tom," she said more loudly. "I know it's you. But I have no clue why you're out here like this wearing a balaclava. What are you doing? Take it off. It looks silly." A moment ago it had been the epitome of masked lovers and rearing horses, passionate clinches and wild rescues. Now it was silly.

"Okay. You're right. It is me. I'm just trying to protect you."

"From what?" She didn't like to say: '*from poo bag pinchers*?' He sounded sulky enough already.

"From people who don't have your best interests at heart, only their own. At this time of year, there are even more hanging around than usual. You shouldn't really be out and about on your own this late on New Year's Day – what with all the pissheads and the people waiting to take advantage."

"Is that why you were loitering around in your car outside my house earlier tonight? Were you protecting me then too?"

"Yes."

Kate sighed heavily and clutched at her temper, desperate not to let it loose. "This can't go on, Tom," she ground out. "You're stalking me and have been since we split up. It's got to stop."

"I'm not stalking you, Kate. I'm just trying to look after you…"

"Yes. You said!" She gripped Rover's lead even tighter and headed for home.

"I'll see you later," he called after her, no longer keeping his voice down to Zorro-like decibels.

She grunted in a decidedly unromantic manner and marched off dragging Rover with her. To add yet another disappointment, Rover kept looking over at Tom as if he would have played throw-the-ball with Rover given half a chance, and as if he wasn't an impostor-Zorro who had just torn all the romance out of her psyche as painfully as if he'd torn an embedded plaster off a deep, deep wound!

It did occur to her to wonder how Tom knew about Zorro. But – maybe he didn't know about Zorro. Maybe it was coincidence that he was hanging around looking like Zorro. To be fair, he looked like a cat burglar, too. He wasn't necessarily *trying* to look like Zorro.

Even if he wasn't, Tom had ruined her whole Zorro-fantasy now and Kate felt decidedly sulky herself.

Chapter Eight

Kate knew she had a black waistcoat somewhere, an old one of Tom's. Going to the dinner tonight as Hans Solo with a four-legged Princess Leia in tow wasn't such a bad idea, and then she could honestly say Rover's balaclava was a costume rather than a disguise. Well, *honestly* enough to suit herself for now, although she felt her principles were slipping badly, but needs must when you've fallen in love with an outlaw, paid off a drug dealer, and went through life with a stolen dog by your side.

Although she had now handed over the dosh for him, she wasn't as convinced as she'd like to be that Rover had actually been Weasel-Face's dog to start with. Kate decided to continue with the Princess Leia charade for the time being or until she could be certain Rover was legally hers.

She telephoned first to make sure it was okay to bring Rover. Thankfully, her dad answered. "No problem, Kate, bring him with you. We have had dogs here before you know."

"Of course we have! Goodness – that was a long time ago." He'd been called Belter because he was incapable of walking anywhere. Nothing slowed that dog down until death brought him to a skidding halt. Kate liked to think he was belting around in the great park in the sky while he waited for his humans to arrive.

"Yes, it was. So it's about time there was another," Dad Benning said.

"Thank you, Dad!"

"Uh. Your mother's feeling a bit starchy about you not showing up last night."

"I really wasn't well enough. I have a stinking cold," Kate said.

"I know. Don't worry about it. But you know the trouble she goes to when it's our turn to host The Three Families' events and she just feels a little unappreciated. I'm just warning you."

"Thanks, Dad. I'll bring flowers."

"That's the ticket. See you soon."

A few hours later, after a bracing shower to wake her up properly, and a final check on Rover to make sure he was as presentable as a Border Collie can be when he's been dyed and made to wear a Princess Leia balaclava, Kate left the house for The Three Families New Year's Day dinner.

Still apprehensive about how this would go, Kate stepped from her car where she'd parked it outside her childhood home. She lifted the boot lid and Rover jumped down. He looked keen. The pair of them walked up the garden path, Kate holding onto the big bouquet of flowers as though she could use it as a shield against motherly wrath.

After the brass ring in the lion's mouth thudded onto its rest, the door was flung open and amidst the sound of Bridget's look-at-me laughter, and the Christmas music that spilled out into the night, Kate stepped forward and hugged her dad.

Wordlessly, they wished each other a Happy New Year. He must be the human she was closest to in all the world. Her throat closed at the thought she was going to disappoint him with her confession about breaking up with Tom, and she pulled back, smiled, and indicated Rover.

"My, he's a handsome feller, isn't he," her father said. "What's his name?" He hunkered down in front of Rover and cradled his head. Kate had forgotten it was her dad who originally brought Belter home for them. It was her mother who had put her foot down and refused the request to get another dog after Belter had gone on to Rainbow Bridge.

"He's called... uh..." Eek! She'd not thought of a name. He was in disguise, a wanted animal, a stolen mutt. She couldn't call him 'Rover'. She couldn't really call him Princess Leia Organa of Alderaan even if he was dressed up as her. He'd end up with identity issues. Also, at some point, someone would probably notice he wasn't a she.

"Sorry, love. What was that? The racket that lot are making is drowning us out a bit." Dad nodded behind him just as a particularly loud crack of laughter announced to Kate that her brother, Pete, was already here. He had one of those laughs that always took you by surprise even when you were expecting it.

"He's, uh, just... uh...jus..." she mumbled, her brain racing around in small circles and getting nowhere.

"Jess? Did you say Jess?" Dad queried, turning back to Rover. "No, you can't have. He's a he. You must have said Jeff." Dad bent to touch noses with Jeff. "What a good dog you are!" He scratched behind Jeff's ears to the dog's intense pleasure and then Dad Benning straightened up again grinning at Kate.

"Look at him," he said. "He doesn't seem at all bothered, does he? Despite all the noise and being in a strange place. I wonder what he'll make of the even stranger people within."

Her dad winked at her and Kate felt an almost overwhelming surge of love for him. Trust her amazing Dad to be so chuffed for her. He was the only one in her life who'd always accepted everything about her just as it was. No question. Even a dog called Jeff. Which was just as good a name as any when all was said and done.

Then her mother, who'd always insisted on being 'Stella' to everyone including her own children, crowded in, throwing kisses at her, grabbing the flowers, and the moment was gone.

Before departing the scene, Stella said, "What on earth is that thing on its head? He looks embarrassed." She waved a wooden spoon at Jeff's knitted fashion accessory and rushed off kitchen-wards without waiting for an answer.

69

Poor old Jeff had been dying to say hello to Stella, but Kate didn't think he looked self-conscious about anything. He was too anxious to get inside, say hello to everyone and share his fur with them. And here she'd been thinking he'd quiver and shake and hide somewhere. He was definitely more sociable than she was!

Kate entered the front room and saw that, as promised, Bridget had got Clark there early, too. Kate smiled. It was good to see him again. He gave her an almost invisible wink. Bridget clung to his arm as if she'd never let it go.

She wore a colourful tunic patterned with zig-zags – the sort of design Kate had to avert her eyes from before a migraine started. A belt around it emphasised her tiny waist. Bridget's long legs were clad in pale gold leggings which led down to gold shoes of a dizzying height. They appeared to totally encase her feet but were punched so full of a filigree pattern it was like a visual illusion. Her tunic was, apparently, all in one piece but for a curious arrangement of cut outs which entirely exposed her shoulders and her cleavage, but somehow it still managed to stay up.

Bridget's long hair, the exact same shade of praline and caramel as Jeff's legs, hung over one shoulder making her look at once innocent and yet, at the same time, the exact opposite. Her face, as ever, was immaculately made up; the smoky eyes and pouting lips currently squinched up for Clark's benefit as she stared into his face and tried to give the world the impression that he was everything to her.

Which meant, at least to Kate, that Spencer Hamilton couldn't be far away. Bridget would be putting on her cringeworthy show of Clark-adulation for her erstwhile fiancé's benefit, no doubt about it.

And there he was, with Mum Hamilton, just coming in from the back as if mother and son had been taking the air outside in the garden. He seemed to be already the worse for wear for drink. Along with his mother…

Goodness! It really did look like Mum Hamilton was drunk, too, the way she was weaving on her feet and hanging onto Spencer as if he was all that was holding her up. It was an alarming picture.

Kate hadn't ever seen Mum Hamilton being anything other than calm and sober and here she was all wild-eyed and ragged.

Dad Hamilton appeared from the direction of the kitchen. No doubt he'd been out and politely offered to help Stella. Who, just as politely, would have refused it. He glared disapprovingly as his son and wife laughed uproariously at something the one had hiccupped into the other one's ear.

Dad Benning hurried over to Dad Hamilton and gave him a drink of something amber whereupon he sat down and twirled his glass on the arm of the sofa as though bored to tears with the proceedings and he only stayed to be mannerly.

Well, that accounted for the Hamilton parents and two of their sons.

At least the Cole parents seemed relatively happy and at ease. From where she sat Kate could see them standing together in the dining room admiring Stella's flower arrangement on the table. By tradition it would have been made entirely from foliage, flowers and berries from the garden.

As Kate stood taking it all in, Tom Cole, her fiancé, but not really her fiancé, arrived with Errol Hamilton. They must have met on the garden path. Kate couldn't imagine they'd arrived together deliberately. They'd always barely managed to be civil to each other. Tom glanced her way and Kate noted the flush that started up his throat, but he ignored her and turned back as if to make an important point to Errol. They both clutched the obligatory bottle of wine which Dad Benning took in charge.

By this time Tom was talking too animatedly to Errol Hamilton, warehouse-dwelling literary writer who'd just 'been passing' in the middle of the night to see if she had a dog... Even though there was nowhere to pass on to from her place. Idly Kate wondered what that was all about.

She was too tired to pursue it, and she was also too tired to try and be friendly with Tom, too. She just wanted to

71

sit quietly and relax. Her dad was busy making people feel welcome and refilling glasses, and Stella would be fiddling with last minute touches in the kitchen. Kate knew better than to see if she could help, so she settled on the smaller sofa, glass of mango and passion fruit sparkly drink in hand, and watched as Jeff made the rounds.

It was good not to have to make conversation for a while. She was happy to observe the assembled company. Most of the people from her childhood were there, The Three Families who had lived alongside each other all these years: her own Benning family, Tom and Bridget's family, the Coles, and the largest family, the Hamiltons, all named for film-stars by movie-fan Mum Hamilton. They had all grown up together. It was a nice feeling of continuity, but had also proved to be a bit stifling over the years.

A commotion in the doorway and an irritatingly tinkly laugh announced the arrival of Marilyn Hamilton. Immediately, Pete Benning's gaze joined with hers as if they'd clicked into place and would be anchored to each other forever. Kate was startled by the intensity of it and wondered how she'd missed the development of that particular relationship.

Marilyn Hamilton wore her hair blonde tonight, with dark roots; it hung in a satiny sheet straight down to her waist. She wore a scarlet sleeveless top belted with a black strip of fabric that matched her shiny black leggings, which were solid black at the back of her legs but lacy at the front. She looked weirdly naked even though, technically, apart from her arms and face, she was covered all over in fabric. Her shoes matched the scarlet of the dinky top; they were open-toed and had a natty little bow on the ankle strap. The heels must have been at least four inches high. How she could walk in them was a complete mystery to Kate who was glad her own less-than-glamorous flatties were covered by a dog.

An uninhibited guffaw pulled Kate's stare away from Marilyn to Mum Hamilton where she and Spencer rocked together in riotous hoots of laughter oblivious, or in spite of, Dad Hamilton's glare.

Mum Hamilton could be the twin of Marilyn only twice her age, sun-baked and leathery, with an intelligence that shone from her in razor-like beams of light too bright to look at for long. Marilyn's brainpower, in contrast, was more like the knife consigned to the shoe-cleaning box for scraping dried mud off one's brogues before polishing them.

Marilyn's tinkling giggles rose an octave as if to ward off her mother's peals of hilarity and Kate looked back at her. Heaven knows what Pete was saying to Marilyn. The way they were looking at each other was wildly inflammatory and wholly unsuited to a family occasion.

After all these years of everyone assuming that the first Three Families wedding would be between Kate and Tom, it might well turn out to be her brother and Marilyn's nuptials on the cards instead.

Kate leaned over to pat Jeff in case he was unsettled by all the noise, but he wasn't there. She spotted him across the room staring intently at Mum Cole, who, unable to resist, bent to talk to him, ruffling his fur and scratching his chest.

That dog had a stare that was almost a physical thing in its own right. He'd been practising it on her, and Kate knew that you could ignore it all you like, but no matter how hard you tried, you could still 'feel' it boring a hole in to you until you gave in and did whatever it was he wanted you to do, which seemed to be just to give him some affection, so it wasn't difficult to obey. Yes, he didn't need to make a sound to get attention – his stare was very, very loud all by itself.

The name 'Jeff' was growing on her, partly because of the squawks of outrage from Bridget and Marilyn when the subject arose and someone said: "Jeff. She's called him Jeff." Kate saw the sideways looks and the smiles that said how stupid a name they thought it for a dog. Well, neither Errol nor Clark thought it stupid, it seemed, and after them she stopped wondering what anyone else thought of it. It was her dog's name. End of.

And her dog didn't mind it, and he was happy to wear his Princess Leia balaclava so she didn't care what snide comments some people might make about that either, although she did wonder if his head might not be getting a bit hot. But it was an essential part of his disguise so she didn't dare take it off. Plus, if it only muted the noise of the inevitable New Year fireworks a little it would help him feel better.

She wished now that she'd had the nerve to dye the white on his head, too, and then she could dispense with the knitwear once all fear of fireworks was past, but it was too late now. She'd know better for next time she stole a dog. She barely stopped herself from snorting with laughter, turning it into a smile as Dad Cole came and sat beside her.

They shared a look. Kate had always liked Tom's father. It made her sad to know that soon she must tell him she'd broken off the engagement with his son. But it had to be done. She didn't want to think about it now. It would have to wait until the appointed time, which was when they had coffee and confections. It had become yet another Three Families tradition to do this at the New Year's Day dinner. People unburdened themselves of all kinds of confessions during it and were forgiven. That was the point – they knew they would be forgiven.

She wasn't entirely sure how the tradition had come about. It started when she was too young to be aware of such things, but had always seemed like a good idea to her. Most things could be forgiven with a good pudding, she reckoned. Or even in exchange for one: *"Please forgive me for sabotaging your hanging baskets in this year's 'Colourful Community Competition', and I'll give you a bowl of Eton mess."*

"Um, no, that won't do, but I'll take the salted caramel chocolate shortbread."

"Done!"

If only that would work for everything!

Looking around at the assembled party, she relaxed a little. It was like a condensed version of her youth in this house tonight.

Kate's determination to reveal her broken engagement wavered. It did seem a shame for anything to spoil this get together. It was so lovely to think The Three Families had continued to do this all these years and every New Year's Day they would come to this dinner and re-strengthen their friendships with each other.

Here they all were together. She might be imagining it, but it was like there was a golden light of warmth and love surrounding them just like an old family fantasy picture painted for a chocolate box. It was very comforting.

Her reverie was interrupted by Marilyn's arrival. She'd managed to unglue herself from Pete. "Hiya, Dad Cole," Marilyn said airily, flicking Dad Cole's cheek as though he was an old school friend rather than one of the parents they'd always looked up to.

Kate had always envied Marilyn her waif-like appearance and the way she moved like she was floating. Kate felt positively solid in comparison. In fact, she felt like a lump... A big, lumpy sort of lump.

"I'm going to think you're talking about some bloke when you say Jeff now," Marilyn said to Kate, skipping away from Jeff's advances. He didn't pursue her. He was obviously a clever dog. He moved onto Dad Cole who seemed relieved to have someone to talk to who only answered back with affection.

Kate wondered how Jeff knew Marilyn didn't want to know him. He'd just accepted it with his usual composure. Maybe there was a different smell about someone who didn't like you. That would certainly be a handy thing.

"I'll be sure to say 'dog' after I say Jeff then," Kate said, deliberately keeping her voice level. "So you don't get confused. As in, 'Jeff-Dog'. Okay? Does that suit you?"

Marilyn shot her a poisonous look which she hastily covered with a flickering of eyelashes and a fluttering of hands. Kate had always been conscious that Marilyn didn't like her, but had no clue why, so she'd given up worrying about it.

Kate looked away from Marilyn to see Jeff-Dog say hello to Pete and was startled to see how her brother reacted. "Get this animal away from me!" he shouted. Jeff-Dog shrank back in fright. Kate jumped to her feet and squared up to Pete.

"Did you hit him?" she demanded before dropping to her knees and putting her arms around Jeff-Dog's neck.

"No, of course I didn't! But I don't want him around me. I don't like dogs."

"This is news," Kate said. "It was you that was always pestering for one when we were young until we got Belter."

"That was then! This is now." He stared at Jeff-Dog, a look of such distaste on his face that Kate shifted around in front of her dog to block the sight of it. She hugged him and whispered, "Never mind. It's only him. You can't expect everyone to love you."

"No. Quite right, too," Clark said. "You can't please all of the people all of the time. And you shouldn't try to."

Kate hadn't noticed him approach and wondered how he'd managed it so quietly with Bridget attached to him like a big, living manacle.

"You're always saying that," Kate said. He was the one out of all of them who could be guaranteed not to toe The Three Families line.

"One day you'll think about it and realise what a piece of genius it is," Clark said, his hand under Jeff-Dog's balaclava scratching behind his ear to the dog's obvious ecstasy. "I didn't know Pete disliked dogs," he added, and Kate wondered why he'd be interested. "Or is it just this one?" he added slowly. Kate had no idea what that meant.

Out of all of them, Pete and Clark had got on the least well. She wondered if Clark felt protective of his half-sister, Marilyn, who used to follow Pete around when little. At that time, Pete would yell at her to go away and he'd run off and leave her behind. He was doing the absolute opposite now.

Not that Kate was objecting. It was none of her business. But maybe Clark didn't like it.

"No, I always thought he liked dogs," she said. "On the other hand, maybe Jeff-Dog will just steer clear now. He has to learn that not everyone is a dog-person, but he is being such a good dog considering the number of people and it all being strange to him."

At which paean of praise Jeff-Dog groaned horribly and fell to the floor with a bone-cracking thump. In terror, Kate followed him down and put her face close to his but soon realised it was bliss which had elicited this reaction, not death. Jeff-Dog was definitely still breathing, his eyes shut, tail twitching, as Clark continued to scratch away at his ears. Jeff-Dog offered him his belly as well, whimpering: *More, more, please, more.*

Kate looked up to see Clark staring in Pete's direction, a questing look on his face that made her uneasy, but Bridget distracted her before she could interrogate him.

"Take the dog away, Kate!" she hissed. "*I* should have Clark's attention just now, not that poxy dog!"

Startled, Kate couldn't think what to say. Bridget was behaving out of character, too. Had everyone been taken over by aliens? She grabbed Jeff-Dog's collar, interrupting his earthly paradise, and walked off with him to an armchair into which she flopped, her trusty hound at her feet.

What was wrong with everyone? Where was the happy family gathering they were so used to? And that only moments ago she'd been imagining. She was conscious of many and varied undercurrents in this house tonight and hadn't a clue what any of them were about. She tried to relax into the back of the armchair. She wished she'd not made the effort to come to this dinner now. Her cold was easily bad enough to be an excuse if she so wished.

In fact, she was going to leave now and to hell with it.

Chapter Nine

As she started to rise, her father perched on the arm of her chair, so she relaxed back again.

"I know what I meant to tell you, Kate. I met my Dutch friend – Bart – do you remember me telling you about him? He does the fishing contests. Anyway, he has over two hundred and sixty different fuchsias where he is just outside Rotterdam and would be delighted if you'd like to go over and see them. You're already a name in fuchsias in Holland. How about that then? I could go with you."

He looked so wistful Kate knew she'd do it. It would be nice for him to have a break from his usual routine, and from her mother. Kate had always wanted to go, anyway, having heard about these fuchsias before, and seen pictures of them.

She and her Dad made some semi-serious arrangements for a trip to Holland which buoyed Kate up so much she decided to stay for the New Year's Day dinner after all, and make the most of her mother's amazing culinary skills.

But by the time they were all seated and the starter served, Kate wondered if she could change her mind again and go home now! She'd never heard The Three Families parents arguing as much as they were tonight. Her own parents were all right as long as her dad didn't say anything at all, apart from the usual pleasantries required of mine host. Any more than that and he was likely to be speared by one of Stella's sarcasms.

The Hamilton parents seemed to be barely talking at all, saving their energies for quaffing wine at an alarming rate. And the Cole parents did nothing but snipe at each other the whole time about something that had happened on Christmas Eve, although no matter how hard she listened she couldn't work out what that was.

Nudging Tom who always sat on her right, and probably would always sit on her right until the end of time regardless of who either of them married, she leant into him and asked: "What's wrong with your lot? What happened on Christmas Eve that was so bad they're still arguing about it now?"

"God knows," he said, his mouth drooping in a way that brought his twelve-year-old self immediately to Kate's mind when he'd fallen out of a tree and crushed his kite to death, or when his ice lolly had slipped off its stick and landed in the mud.

She gripped his arm. "They'll be all right," she said. "They always are. They all always are." As she said it, she looked around the table and doubted her own words. It was as though nothing but negativity and crossness filled the room. Surely she wasn't imagining it!

"Not this time, I don't think," he said, finally turning to look at her. She wanted to put her arms around him like she used to, and hug him until things got better. She knew it would be a mistake, though. He would somehow turn it into meaning they should be getting married. So she held back. "I've never known them be so bitter," he added. "I think they're going to break up."

"Oh no! That's awful. Bridget hasn't mentioned it."

"Huh!" he snorted at mention of his sister. "She's probably not even noticed. She's such a self-centred little bitch!"

"What?" Kate squeaked. They never talked about each other like this.

"You heard me. And you know it's true. Or you would, if you ever looked around you at what's actually going on in the real world, instead of always hiding your

79

head, concentrating on little pots of compost and cuttings and rooting powder yada yada."

"I don't use rooting powder," Kate said slowly, after which no words came to her mind at all. It was unlike Tom to be bitter and she wished with everything she had that it wasn't her that had made him so.

She stared down at two starters that had appeared on her plate – the Stilton and pear toast with watercress her dad liked so much, and the mini twice-baked herby salmon soufflé Stella preferred. She poked them with her fork, but her appetite had fled.

She wished she had gone home. Her hands dropped to her lap and were immediately filled with a dog's head. She was so grateful at the instant love and immense comfort it brought that she wanted to kiss Jeff-Dog, but it was anatomically impossible to get at him without making people sitting both sides of her move, and she didn't want to draw any attention to herself. It strengthened her resolve to confess to their broken engagement and be done with this messing around. She would feel bad if she hurt Tom but some things just had to be done.

Briefly she wondered if anyone would notice if she got under the table with her dog. She'd be much happier with just him for company. And if that was cowardly or hiding her head, then so be it.

"As for you," Tom continued. "You were too ill to come out last night to the party, but you still managed to be not ill enough to go out and get a dog. Not to mention nearly smashing into me when you did so."

"If I had smashed into you, it would have served you right. Why were you spying on me?"

"I wanted to make sure you were all right," Tom said, concentrating hard on his plate.

Kate stared at the side of his head. What a weird thing to say. He'd said it before and it had sounded odd then, too. What did he mean? Or was her feverish and over-active mind seeing everything as weird?

While she stared at him her gaze travelled down his arm to his cuffs. He wasn't wearing the tell-tale Jaguar cufflinks! That must be the first time she had ever seen him in shirt cuffs but without her cufflinks holding them together. A lump suddenly appeared in her throat and she tried hard not to sob for what they'd lost.

Raised voices percolated through her misery. Or at least, one raised voice. It was Pete's. It *would* be Pete's. Her brother was another who seemed rather the worse for alcoholic wear. He wasn't the most reserved of people at the best of times, but he certainly wasn't holding back now.

Kate peered around Tom's shoulder to see who Pete was shouting at, and was horrified to see that it was Marilyn's dad. For some reason Dad Hamilton was on the receiving end of Pete's ire even though he was the most laid back person in the whole of the Western hemisphere and people never fell out with him.

Pete must be really drunk. Why wasn't someone holding him down or gagging him?

Clark started to his feet and advanced around the table. Pete jumped up to face him. Kate could understand Clark not wanting anyone to yell at his step-father, but she really hoped he wasn't going to hit her brother. Pete spent most of the time when he was around irritating the hell out of her, but he was still her brother. She rose from her chair, but found herself anchored in place by Tom's hand.

"What do you think you're doing?" she hissed at him.

"Keeping you out of trouble," he said.

"I can get in trouble if I want to!" she snapped.

The look he gave her made her want to sink her teeth into his hand where it was clamped onto her arm, but she managed to restrain herself. She had a dog to think about and, annoyingly, she knew he was right. Pete wouldn't thank her for rushing to his rescue.

When she looked back to that end of the table it was just in time to hear Marilyn yell at Clark: "You're not my real brother! This is none of your business."

Whoa! That was a bit naff. Even for Marilyn.

81

Clark's face darkened but before he could say anything, Errol had leapt into the fray too. "Well I *am* your 'real' brother," he said. "And you're just a silly girl if you want to be involved with him." And he threw a punch at Pete who went down like a sack of rocks. Errol looked at his knuckles in surprise as if to say *'how did that happen?'* and turned to Dad Hamilton. "Sorry, Dad. I know you're perfectly capable of looking after yourself, but I also know you need to look after your hands for your work. I don't, though."

By this time Pete had come round, struggled to his feet and lunged at Errol, but Clark deflected him and he fell to the floor again, Marilyn uttering little shrieks and getting in the way of anyone who wanted to help or hinder him.

Dad Benning had arrived at the scene. Kate had seen her mother mouthing at him from the other end of the table and nodding towards the ruckus before he muttered something and rose slowly to his feet.

He helped his son to a standing position and said something to him so softly no one else could hear. Kate saw the murderous look on Pete's face and how her father's features hardened in response in an expression she didn't think she'd ever seen on him before. Her father grabbed Pete's arm and they left the room together, Pete obviously going whether he wanted to or not. Kate was gobsmacked. Her father was never that inflexible. Looking back at her mother, she was shocked to see Stella stricken and mute.

What the hell was going on?

She was interested to note that Tom and Bridget's parents – Mum and Dad Cole – plus Bridget, and Spencer, had left the table and gathered together on the sofa as though distancing themselves from it all. She wondered if that meant Bridget and Spencer were back together again.

At the other end of the room, Mum and Dad Hamilton, looking anxious, clung together murmuring softly.

Their New Year's Day dinner party that they'd all had together for the last twenty-eight years, starting four years before Kate was even born, had disintegrated into rubble.

Despite this, when her mother shouted, "Dinner is served!" into the mounting tension, everyone, including Pete and his father, came back to the table as though nothing untoward had occurred, sat in their designated places and started passing each other the vegetables.

Her mother served up her own special version of the lamb, lentils, loads of garlic and sun-dried tomatoes dish which was unmissable no matter what catastrophes were taking place. A series of mumbled "Thank you, Stella," were the only words Kate could hear as everyone lapsed into their own thoughts and dug in. This was the very essence of comfort-food in a world gone mad.

There was more eating noise than usual, more sounds of cutlery hitting crockery, less chatter and laughs than usual, but they were still all there. Only this time Kate wondered how much of it was a facade and not the real thing. But then, maybe it had never been a real thing and she hadn't realised.

She'd hate to think her idyllic childhood had all been a big sham, although gaining new knowledge after the event didn't change the event itself.

Watching her brother, Kate frowned. What was all that about? Why would Pete have a go at Marilyn's father? At least Pete's appetite appeared undimmed, so whatever it was couldn't be that bad. Could it?

Marilyn herself was so entwined with Pete it was difficult to tell where he began and she ended so her lover's disagreement with her father wasn't souring her ardour.

Kate began to feel apprehensive about confession time. How many of The Three Families members had things to confess this year? There was usually quite a good crop of revelations, most of which they could laugh about by the time they'd reached that stage of the meal.

How many people would laugh about the demise of her engagement to Tom? She had a sinking feeling that her confession might be one of the ones that people politely listened to, but then they'd turn away and start talking about something else as though she'd said nothing.

The tradition was that anything confessed on this special occasion was always forgiven, but some things had been received in such a way Kate knew that although they might never be mentioned again in the spirit of the tradition, they wouldn't truly be forgiven. It was almost enough to put her off her food.

Clutching Jeff-Dog's ear more firmly, she turned to Tom. "Have you the faintest idea what's going on?"

"You and I split up. That was enough to put the kibosh on last year, wasn't it," he said softly, but he held his hands up in surrender at her look. "You meant about Pete, didn't you," he said in his normal voice. "Pete's had to leave the police force because he was on the take. But then, he's only your brother. You couldn't be expected to know this, what with your cuttings and your flower shows and all."

His sniping had no effect on her. If at that moment an abyss opened up in the dining room floor and they all fell in, she wouldn't notice that either.

"But, Pete," she said slowly. "Pete on the take? Pete's not on the take..."

A pained look on his face, Tom turned fully to face her. "I'm sorry, Kate. I had to..." but he didn't get the chance to finish what he was going to say before Marilyn yelled: "Of course he isn't!" Kate flinched. Goodness. She hadn't said it that loudly had she?

"Take that back, Tom," Marilyn demanded, wild-eyed, looking ready to do someone a damage.

Tom said nothing.

Errol leaned across the table, staring at his sister. "You're right, Marilyn. He's not on the take," he said. "Or not any more. He's been kicked off the force, so he *can't* take any more. Or, he could, still, I suppose, literally speaking. No. Okay. My mistake. He's still on the take." He leant back again, a cold glitter in his eyes and a half-smile on his face that reminded Kate of a stuffed crocodile she'd seen in the museum when she was small. It gave her nightmares for months and resulted in her getting her own night-light.

Marilyn's chair flew over backwards as she jumped up and lunged, her fingers curved like claws, at her brother, but he easily held her off, much to her spitting and cursing rage.

It was all just background noise to Kate. "Surely not," she protested again shaking her head. She couldn't imagine any offspring of her parents being dishonest. As she thought it, she caught her breath considering her own dishonesty about how she got her dog. But that wasn't on a par with a policeman being 'on the take', whatever that meant. Her brother was a corrupt policeman? No, she couldn't take it in.

"But how did he get caught, even if he was?" she asked.

"Information," Errol said flatly, still keeping a struggling Marilyn at bay, but easily speaking over her. "Information was laid against him. He was protecting drug dealers and some people can't stomach that even if they're prepared to turn a blind eye to other stuff."

"I suppose that was you as well!" Marilyn hissed.

"Unfortunately, no, but if I'd known about it – it certainly would have been. You can bank on that."

"But it's Pete," Kate said. "Our Pete."

"And 'your Pete' is still present," Pete said dryly. He took another mouthful of lamb and appeared to ignore the rumpus. No one else was still eating. It was as if they'd been caught in a powerful beam of light and frozen in place.

"I know," Errol said. "Being one of ours doesn't make him a saint, Kate. And I've seen what drugs can do to a person so I have no sympathy. I'm sorry, but there it is."

Next to her, Tom stroked his hand down Kate's arm as though that would make her feel better. It made her feel worse. She couldn't believe her brother was guilty of such a charge; nor could she believe his 'family' which comprised The Three Families, were turning against him in this way. How could they possibly believe it?

They were supposed to be in 'safe' company when they were all together. They all knew each other, had grown up together and trusted each other. They could all depend on each other if needed. Or that had been the idea, she thought. And yet, no one was jumping to Pete's defence. Glancing at him she tried a little smile but he looked through her.

"So that's what the altercation was about earlier. Dad Hamilton was objecting to his daughter being so closely associated with a corrupt cop," Tom said. "And Pete was objecting to his objections."

"You don't think Pete is capable of this do you?" Kate asked. Somehow if Tom thought it then it would be a lot worse.

Another flare-up from Marilyn and Errol claimed most people's attention. Under cover of this renewed outburst Tom looked around as if checking to see if anyone could hear him, leaned in closer to her and whispered, "No, I don't. I think there's something going on and we're just getting the tip of the iceberg which is throwing us off the scent of what's really happening."

Chapter Ten

Kate stared at Tom and he nodded to her as if to underline his words.

She felt a little better for it, and then the puddings appeared and she felt a lot better. They were all home-made of course. They were Stella-made as well, which guaranteed the most yumminess. While such puddings existed in the world, life couldn't be that bad. If she really concentrated on the puddings everything else would get better. In her mind a caped hero saluted her from the back of his rearing horse.

Her grandmother's special antique art deco opalescent glass dish arrived full of Stella's tiramisu. Such bliss! How was it possible that bad things lurked in the same room as this tiramisu? Virtuously, Kate held back, but her incredible restraint was severely tested by the arrival of the most gloriously-smelling caramel confection to ever grace the Flemish point lace that currently clothed the Benning household's dining table. How she remained in her seat would forever be a mystery to her.

Thankfully, next out was a fruit salad. A luxurious fruit salad, no doubt about that, but a fruit salad nevertheless, which was such a very healthy idea that she scorned it immediately. She'd leave that to the diet-conscious types who hopefully would eat loads of it and leave more of the really good stuff for her.

No one was doing anything about the delicacies arranged around the table, so Kate took advantage of the lull. She nudged Tom until he passed her a bowl and she helped herself to a big spoonful of tiramisu, poured on double cream and took a mouthful. Ahhh, the bliss.

A commotion the other side of Tom barely registered with her – a really good pudding deserved complete focus. But the noise got louder and louder and finally she glanced up to see Dad Cole had left his seat next to her and moved to the other side of Tom where Mum Hamilton sat. Kate was conscious that Tom held himself rigidly still as if movement would break him.

Now what was going on? Reluctant to find out, Kate took another mouthful of tiramisu and screwed up her face in ecstasy, but Tom's words about how she always retreated into her own world and ignored everyone else's forced her to grudgingly open her eyes and start to take note of events.

Across the table from her, Dad Hamilton was glaring at his wife. He had a finger pointed at Dad Cole in a way that could only be described as 'accusing'. Dad Hamilton was absolutely rat-arsed so no one could be sure quite what point he was making. And yet, people were reacting. Dad Cole still stood protectively at Mum Hamilton's shoulder.

The entire room was motionless and quiet and waiting. Everyone, except Kate, knew something was going on. She took another spoonful of pudding, but then had great difficulty swallowing it. It didn't want to go down, and when it did, the noise it made seemed to echo around the room. Not wanting to make such a racket with her eating and disturb the scene that apparently was about to play out, she carefully placed her spoon down on her plate and paid close attention to the drama playing out before her.

Dad Hamilton continued to glare at his wife and point at Dad Cole.

Tom still didn't move.

No one said a word.

So, of course, Kate had to cough and it was the kind of cough that the harder she tried to hold it back the worse it made her throat tickle and the more coughs forced themselves through her reluctant throat. It seemed to unlock the tableau, though, and when she'd recovered, after a hefty thwack on the back from someone near and a drink of water, the level of noise in the room had risen to almost thundering. Which didn't help her understand what was going on any more than the silence had.

Eventually, Mum Cole's hysterical voice pierced the commotion but, after a childhood spent becoming accustomed to it, alarm wasn't Kate's first reaction. Mum Cole could get overwrought about the diseases that awaited children who didn't do their jackets right up to their throats, not to mention what could happen if you tracked mud across a clean floor – people could slip on it, break their ribs and puncture their lungs. The world had always been an especially scary place for Mum Cole.

But this time Kate wondered if Tom's mother was right to be worked up. It seemed that there'd been hanky-panky going on between Dad Cole and Mum Hamilton. Kate was so stunned at the idea that she spent some time trying to imagine she was in bed at home lost in a feverish hallucination, because this couldn't possibly be true. But Jeff-Dog's cold nose on her ankle brought her back to earth and she had to believe that it *was* true.

She stared at Mum Cole and remembered other scenes from her childhood – the day a prison break was announced on the radio and The Three Families children had not told anyone they were riding their bikes down to the fields where perverts were bound to be hiding in the bulrushes, batting away iridescent dragonflies and frightening the fish while they waited to snatch up children and do unspeakable things to them.

Kate remembered Mum Cole racing towards them when she realised where they'd gone, wild hair flying, her husband's cricket bat in hand, totally ready to protect them against escaped prisoners with her bare hands if necessary.

Mum Cole also made the absolutely best ice lollies ever, using plastic lolly-shaped moulds with sticks that you could unroll into a single sheet of paper after you'd eaten the lolly. This fascinated Kate, although then she never knew what to do with the paper.

How was it possible that Dad Cole and Mum Hamilton would even think to cheat on Mum Cole?

Mum Cole made a keening noise and fled the room.

"Is this really, true, Dad?" Bridget asked.

"What do you think?" Dad Cole sounded positively belligerent about it.

Tom's shoulders got even higher. He'd rub his ears off his head soon. Kate laid her hand on his arm in an unthinking gesture of solidarity, but his flinch as though she'd burnt him made her hastily remove it and replace it on Jeff-Dog's head. Jeff-Dog was getting his head rubbed so much Kate wouldn't be surprised to find him bald when he finally came out from under the table and took his balaclava off.

"Mum?" Marilyn shrieked across the table to her mother. The Hamilton boys remained silent. Kate peered around Tom to see Mum Hamilton nodding her head but not looking at anyone.

So it was true.

"Did you know about this?" she whispered to Tom.

"No, not really. I knew something was going on, but I had no idea it was this." He looked so stunned that Kate nearly put her hand back on his arm but remembered herself in time and didn't.

Really, she was being completely outclassed here. She couldn't think why she'd been worried. A broken engagement and a spot of dog-stealing weren't even in the running. In fact, they were so insignificant they probably weren't even worth mentioning. People would think she was wasting their time. Not that she was going to mention about the dog-napping anyway, but the guilt of it did weigh heavy. She wouldn't have done any different, though. She couldn't imagine leaving Jeff-Dog behind on his own in that place with that awful man and fireworks going off all the time when he was on his own and frantic.

She felt heartless thinking about her own affairs in the middle of the chaos overtaking The Three Families around her. A thing like Mum Hamilton and Dad Cole having an

90

affair couldn't happen in isolation. They would all be traumatised by it. Kate would like to ignore it, but knew she couldn't. Her whole life seemed to be dissolving around her into a mess on the floor. All the things that had always seemed so solid and enduring had become flimsy and transient.

But, no matter how trivial in comparison, although she mustn't let Tom know that she thought it trivial, she had to confess about breaking off their engagement so that people no longer expected them to get married. It wasn't fair on them, or on her because it also meant she couldn't live her own life properly. Why Zorro should come to mind at that point she had no idea! Her original Zorro, that was! Not the impostor Zorro with the Jaguar cufflinks...

"Have some pudding," she said. "This tiramisu is delicious."

Tom gave her such a look that she snatched at the tiramisu herself and put far too much on her plate. Damn. Now she'd have to eat it. Her mother would never forgive her if she took all that and then left some.

"Um, what's happening? I mean, the fact that they've come clean about all this – does this mean they're going to set up house together or what? And why have they confessed if it comes to it? I mean, how long's it been going on for?"

But her mother's strident voice drowned out any reply Tom might have given. "Honestly, Mum Hamilton," Stella said. "You could have waited until the traditional confession time instead of spoiling people's desserts." Stella clearly believed wholesale adultery and family dissolution quite unworthy of such attention when her puddings languished unloved and uneaten.

Or maybe, Kate thought, as she watched her mother, maybe she was trying to avoid it all, too. Gosh, fancy thinking her mother had doubts and insecurities! That was weird, but also strangely comforting. Here she was thinking about stolen dogs and how on earth she was going to get her engagement ring off when the end of the betrothal was finally made public, and there was her mother thinking about unappreciated puddings.

For the first time in her life Kate felt as though she and her mother might in fact be members of the same species. A strange feeling of kinship enveloped her as she watched Stella.

She was a very determined woman, her mother. Stella, intolerant of the lack of response, snatched up the caramel mousse ganache yummy confection and went around the table slamming spoonfuls of it down on to plates. Those who knew better than to take some of Stella's pudding and then not eat it, and who were quick enough, avoided future trouble by covering their plates with their hands. Even in the middle of all this drama people's sense of self-preservation was still obviously to the fore.

Despite observing it in others, Kate didn't think to cover her own plate in time, and gazed in despair at the extra pile of pudding her mother plonked on it. She'd already eaten her own bodyweight in tiramisu, and now she had to force this down to show her loyalty to her mother.

And there was still the coffee and her mother's array of home-made petits-fours and other delicacies to get through and, of course, the official confession time. God only knew what horrors awaited although Kate couldn't help feeling that they must, surely, pale into insignificance compared to what had already gone before. She felt sick to think of it.

Kate knew her duty. She picked up her spoon and ploughed through the pudding. Although all sense of taste had disappeared, she must stuff this pudding into a space no longer roomy enough to accommodate it peacefully. And then be up all night with the consequences. Not even Jeff-Dog could help. It had a little chocolate in it and she knew human chocolate was bad for dogs but had no idea how much was needed to be lethal. It might be a tiny bit for all she knew so she couldn't risk dropping any of it into her lap for him to dispose of.

Talking of Jeff-Dog. It surely must be time for him to need the lawn. It would give Kate an opportunity to stretch out her stomach as well, make its contents spread around a little further and hopefully ease the congestion going on in there.

"Where are you going?" Tom wanted to know.

"I'm just taking Jeff-Dog outside for a moment."

"I'll come with you."

"There's no need!" she said, but he rose to his feet anyway. "I can make it out onto my own parents' lawn unaided, you know!" What was it with him? This need to constantly keep her in sight. It was very irritating. She gritted her teeth. She'd have to tolerate it because he was having such a rotten time with his family.

No one made any comment about them leaving the dining room, which in itself was unusual for such a nosy crowd of people, but just went to show what a very odd New Year's Day dinner they were having.

Chapter Eleven

They went through the kitchen and the back door to the garden outside. It was very, very dark, the moon obscured by heavy cloud, a light wind whispering in the trees.

Jeff-Dog raced out onto the lawn, but couldn't decide where to sniff first and ran around in little circles before hunkering down.

"I am so sorry, Tom," Kate said. "About your parents. I can only imagine how you must feel."

His figure was solid beside her but his face was all shadows and she couldn't see his expression. "I don't believe it," he said.

Denial, Kate thought. Understandable.

"And it's not denial," Tom continued as if he could read her thoughts. "I simply don't believe it. They're lying. The puzzle is – why are they lying?"

How ridiculous! The parents wouldn't lie about something like that! Kate didn't want to argue with Tom just now so she patted his arm consolingly. He jerked away from her. "They are lying, Kate! Just because you don't want to think that our parents would lie – let me tell you – they lie all the time!"

Kate didn't know what to say or do that wouldn't result in a flaming row. She gazed about her, not that she could see much in the shifting gloom. Except that she *could* see something – something flitting between the trees – a darker shadow than the ones around it.

Was it Zorro? What a pity Zorro's modern counterpart didn't wear that distinctive flat brimmed hat. That would make it much easier to identify him in silhouette and she could be more sure when it was him, and when it was not him. Balaclavas made everyone look the same.

She couldn't understand what had possessed Zorro to turn up here and now, though. She had to distract Tom so he didn't spot him. At least she could be certain it wasn't Tom this time!

"Let's go in. I need a poo bag," she said, clutching at his arm and cringing inside. What spark of genius made her come up with that idea?

"I don't think you need worry about picking up dog poo when we're still in the middle of dinner," Tom said.

"I think I should. I don't want to forget it and then Dad get a nasty surprise tomorrow when he trundles out here with his early morning cup of tea like he does."

"That is a point, I suppose," Tom said absently. He was staring intently over her shoulder. "Did you hear something then?" he asked. "You know, I think there's someone out there. Watching us."

"Nah. Don't be daft," Kate said, conscious she was talking very loudly. "There won't be anyone there. Everyone's too busy celebrating the New Year to be skulking around other people's gardens."

"No, I think there is," Tom said, pushing her towards the house. "Go and get your poo bags and stay in there. Now!"

"No!"

"Now is not the time to argue!" His words were muffled as he disappeared into the rhododendron bushes.

"Nooo…" Kate cried. How could she stop Tom from catching Zorro?

But she didn't need to worry. A sharp, excited canine yelp, wild human cursing and the sounds of people thrashing around in the undergrowth accompanied by the sharp cracking of branches, told her that Jeff-Dog and Tom had fallen over each other in the shrubbery. If Zorro hadn't got away by now he didn't deserve to.

It couldn't be Zorro anyway. He surely wouldn't be lurking in the undergrowth while she was out here with her dog by her side and her nearly-ex. He was Zorro. He would know he wasn't needed just now because he always knew when he *was* needed.

Kate ran indoors so that Tom could recover his dignity without knowing she'd witnessed the loss of it. While there, she collected poo bags and a torch. Cautiously stepping back outside, she found Jeff-Dog and Tom sitting side by side on one of the wooden benches in the patio area. They appeared to be communing like an old married couple sharing reminiscences. He was a very comforting dog, Jeff-Dog. He radiated affection. From her own experience a hug from him had the warmth and recuperative powers of a Mediterranean cruise. She was glad he was there for Tom.

Switching on the torch Kate headed for the spot she wanted to clear, but no matter how hard she looked she couldn't find anything to put in the poo bag. Which was impossible. She'd seen it and she'd marked the spot in her mind. She knew this garden very well and knew exactly where it should be. And it wasn't there.

So where the hell was it? Someone else must have picked it up.

Which was plain silly.

She joined her nearly-ex-fiancé and her dog on the bench, sandwiching Jeff-Dog in between them.

"Did you pick up the poo?" she asked Tom.

"No. You were getting poo bags. Why would I pick it up without?"

"Uh. No reason," she said lamely, unwilling to pursue a really silly conversation.

He shrugged. "I know you said you were going to announce the end of our engagement, Kate," he said. "I wish you wouldn't. Can it wait a few weeks?"

"What is the point of waiting a few weeks?"

"Things will have calmed down a bit, that's all. After all the revelations we've already had tonight and there will be more – we haven't even reached official confession time yet – I don't think we need that as well."

"I don't see that my confession should be any less valid than anyone else's."

"Of course it isn't less valid. It's just one more that might not be necessary on top of everything else."

The tone of his voice got through to her. "Do you know something I don't?" she asked.

"Yes."

What the hell did that mean?

Kate and Jeff-Dog looked up at Tom as he rose from the seat, but he said no more. He held out his arm and Kate took it, resigned to getting no other explanation, but feeling a bit bolshie all the same about him trying to stop her from telling The Three Families their engagement was off. Not to mention not telling her what he knew that she didn't.

The three of them walked inside and headed for the dining room, Kate firmly pushing from her mind the Mystery of the Missing Poo.

Chapter Twelve

They regained their seats and Jeff-Dog settled under the table as though it was a habit of long-standing. Sighing heavily he appeared to fall asleep. He wasn't much of a guard dog, come to think of it. He did nothing when she was mugged and had her bag nicked. On the other hand, what dog in his right mind would want to take down a mugger who'd just stolen his poo? So maybe he'd deliberately done nothing and merely thought it was a good way to get shot of it.

Kate straightened up to face her friends and neighbours again. As she and Tom settled into their chairs and retrieved their serviettes, Stella appeared at the end of the table, Dad Benning just behind his wife holding an enormous tray with coffee pots, cream, cups and all the necessary paraphernalia including plates of home-made petits-fours, chocolate orange truffles, Italian soft nougat and coconut ice squares.

This was the signal for confession time. The fact that some people had jumped the gun on it this year was beside the point. There would always be this time for admitting their wrongs at The Three Families New Year's Day dinner. This tradition would go on until the world exploded. And this time Kate actually had something to confess herself. She was still dithering about whether she should fall in with Tom's wishes to keep quiet – or not.

With her mouth full of truffle, she tugged on her engagement ring as if to take it off. She already knew she was going to have trouble, but she did need to give it back to

Tom. The jewel in it was the size of Hawaii. She was surprised she hadn't been ambushed when she'd gone into the Badlands for Jeff-Dog, or Rover as he was then. The light that shone out of the diamond was like an enormous, flashing beacon inviting muggers to grab it. Or maybe it only looked really flashy to her…

A prolonged I'm-trying-to-get-your-attention coughing made her look up. Kate was held still by a thick silence laden with anticipation. What could possibly be confessed now that could hold the interest after what had gone before?

"I'm pregnant!" Marilyn announced.

"Whose is it?" Stella asked. Straight for the throat.

"It's your Pete's of course!" Marilyn replied, pouting.

"There's no 'of course' about it from what I've seen," Stella retorted.

"Mum!" Pete frowned at his mother and shook his head.

"Now, luv," Dad Benning said. He held his hand up as if to say 'Stop!' but his expression said he'd lost this particular fight already.

Which he probably had, Kate thought. No one was good enough for Stella's son, and certainly not Marilyn, who had never been one of Stella's favourites. Kate eyed Marilyn curiously. Everything about her and her outfit was perfect and lovely, but it was all skin-tight, if not painted on. Kate couldn't work out where a baby, even a baby the size of a peanut, could possibly be hiding. Even a baby the size of a *shelled* peanut would show in that outfit…

"Well, there *is* no 'of coursh', is there?" Dad Hamilton said, unexpectedly providing support for his hostess.

Goodness knows how he'd even taken in what was happening with his daughter after his wife's extra-marital antics had been made public, not to mention taking on board almost an entire bottle of bitter-orange liqueur.

"There'sh no 'of coursh' about it," he slurred again. "Marilyn does sheem to have tried out quite a few firsht. I thought she'd have settled on Tom by now. Oh, shorry, Kate," he said turning his head towards her but appearing to look over her shoulder. "Of coursh, not while engaged to you. But she did try him out." He took another swig from his glass, realised it was empty, and reached for the bottle. "No harm in that," he muttered. "Good idea to try out for shize firsht. As it were."

Oh! Open-mouthed, Kate turned to Tom who stared straight ahead, but a tell-tale flush of blood crept up his neck. Finally forcing her vocal cords to work she hissed, "You had it off with Marilyn?"

"Dad!" Marilyn shouted. "You're pissed. Just shut up!"

But Dad Hamilton wasn't to be stopped now he'd started. He addressed Kate: "Coursh he did. How could she have it off with him without him having it off wiv her? Shilly Billy," he hooted, and rocked backwards and forwards in his chair like a demented tumbler doll. "Like mother like daughter," he added, a wavering toast of his glass in Mum Hamilton's direction which she acknowledged with a startlingly poisonous glare.

"Ohmigod! The high and mighty Tom Cole who can do no wrong has double-crossed his fiancée," Bridget shouted, delighted to get one over on her brother.

"I did *not* double-cross my fiancée!" Tom snapped.

Kate took the unexpected cue she'd been given. "Too late!" she cried. "The trust is gone. I'm ending our engagement right now!" She tugged at the ring and tugged some more, but she couldn't make it budge. She gave it another try. "That's it. I've had it with this engagement. It is no more. Oh, no. No more." It was no good. The blasted ring wasn't coming off.

"Uh," she muttered in a softer tone to Tom, "I'll give you back your ring when I can get it off." She tugged theatrically at it again to demonstrate the point, and added in a whisper: "There, that wasn't so bad was it? Much better than me telling the truth."

All in all, she was pretty chuffed with herself for finding Tom such a great way out. Much better to end like this in a blaze of glory than tell the assembled crowd she'd finished it three months ago.

However, when she looked up at him, he didn't look at all grateful!

Honestly, you tried your best for people and they just didn't appreciate you! She scowled back at him.

"On the other hand," Dad Hamilton said. "Pete'sh good. Pete'sh okay."

"A dodgy policeman! I don't think so!" That was Errol Hamilton, indignation on behalf of his sister rife in his voice.

"Did I hear correctly, Kate?" Stella queried. "Did you just break off your engagement to Tom over an old affair?"

"Selfish cow." That was Bridget chiming in; her best friend who was soon to be demoted from that position.

"Yes. That's right. I don't want someone who can't keep it in his trousers," Kate said airily, snatching up some soft nougat, stuffing it in her mouth and then shaking her head whilst pointing at her bulging cheeks to explain her lack of response to further enquiries, none of which sounded as though they were going to be too friendly.

Really, why did people care given all the other things they had to chew over? She snorted at her own pun and squashed in more nougat, pointing at herself even more frantically, clearly saying that her teeth were stuck together and she couldn't possibly join in their banter.

"It happened a long time before we got together. You know that don't you," Tom said under his breath.

She couldn't understand why he cared. More to the point she couldn't understand why *she* did, but she was pleased to hear it. "Of course I do," she said in her mind, unable to open her mouth for the sticky confectionery glueing it shut. He evidently got the message, though, and flashed her a quick smile before replacing it with his I'm-clearly-grim expression and turning back to face the assembled company.

"I'm disappointed, Kate," Stella said. "Honestly, it's difficult to know how your mind works."

Kate was fairly certain that Pete's disgrace was overwhelming Stella's reaction to her broken engagement and for once in her life she was grateful to her brother for taking all her mother's attention. She glanced at her dad and received an encouraging smile. He would always support her no matter what she decided. A nudge on her legs reminded her that Jeff-Dog would too. She leaned under the table and gave him a quick hug.

When she surfaced it was to find that Bridget was still at it, although she'd changed tack somewhat. "Why couldn't you give us some good news instead of this? Talk about selfish. I thought you were going to give us a wedding date – something nice to look forward to."

"What about your own wedding date? Why can't we look forward to that instead?" Kate said, taking the opportunity of her empty mouth. She had every intention of filling it again forthwith and stretched a hand out for the coconut ice squares on their very pretty blue and white plate.

"Or what about Marilyn's announcement?" she continued. "We have a baby to look forward to and they might get married as well. More good things to look forward to. Why aren't we celebrating that instead of sniping at each other?"

"I can't give a wedding date yet. Spencer won't commit us to one," Bridget said, pouting as she turned to her betrothed. So their little contretemps *had* been resolved, Kate was glad to note. "See, Spencer. People want to know when we're getting married."

Spencer looked uncomfortable. "The trouble is, My Sweet, we could name a date now if you didn't want such an enormously expensive wedding. As it is, I don't know how we're going to afford what you *do* want so I don't know when we can have it. Why don't we name a date now and to hell with it?"

"But I want it to be the best day of my life," Bridget said.

"Won't it be the best day of your life because you're marrying the man you love?" Kate enquired around a mouthful of confection so sweet her teeth ached. "It's not supposed to be the best day of your life because you've spent a fortune you don't have."

"You've never been romantic like me," Bridget retorted.

"And thank heaven for that!"

"I think Spencer might have other reasons for not naming a wedding day, haven't you?" Tom said, his voice heavy.

"What could I possibly have to confess?" Spencer asked his business partner and best friend, a look on his face that dared Tom to answer him.

Tom's face remained rigidly blank. "You know you're supposed to confess your own stuff. It's not about other people telling tales on you. It's about how you take responsibility for yourself. So man up and get on with it."

"What does he mean?" Bridget asked Spencer.

"I don't know," Spencer said, but Kate could see beads of sweat on his brow, and the way he loosened his tie spoke of his unease.

Now what! She clutched more tightly to Jeff-Dog's ear. How could there possibly be anything else?

Bridget was jumping up and down in her seat. "Oh, come on! What is it?" she squeaked, obviously thinking Spencer's confession was going to be some nice surprise to do with her. Everything had to be about her, didn't it!

But Kate didn't think it was going to be about Bridget, judging by the way Tom and Spencer were eyeballing each other. From her vantage point by his side, she could see that Tom's hands were balled into fists on his lap. Something was seriously astray. She was almost afraid to move in case she set something off, some huge explosive device that would detonate in the Benning's dining room and destroy what little was left of their decades-long familial bonding.

But even remaining statue-like, and barely breathing, wasn't going to stop it despite Spencer, too, remaining silent. Kate wondered if she was imagining it, but it seemed to her that Spencer's muteness was sodden with grief.

Tom sighed and flexed his fingers, then clenched them into fists again. "I know you've been swindling the books. How could you possibly think I wouldn't know? I can only assume you wanted me to know, which must mean you want our partnership to end. I would much rather you'd invited me out to the pub for a pint or two and said to me that you wanted the partnership to end. That way we could have terminated our business relationship, but we could have kept our friendship."

The hurt in his voice made Kate let go of Jeff-Dog's ear and clasp her hand over Tom's fist nearest to her, although she thought he hadn't noticed. He was so intent on Spencer she thought the roof could cave in and he would be unaware.

Spencer's face drained of colour; his eyes and mouth opened wide in horror. "No, no! You've got it all wrong! The last thing I want to lose is your friendship. I don't want to lose the partnership either, but if I must, then I must. But not your friendship. Don't say that. I am so sorry." He rubbed his face furiously leaving ragged red marks to stand out on the white. "I've been so stupid. I just didn't know what else to do. I can't believe how stupid I've been."

Kate felt sorry for him. He sounded so bewildered. It was almost as though he didn't know how he'd come to do the swindling.

"Are you sure it was Spencer?" she ventured.

"Who else could it be?" Tom snapped.

"What about one of the accountants you employ. Couldn't it be one of them?"

"No," Spencer said, his head hanging so low down his chest, his chin skimmed the surface of his coffee. "It was me. I am so sorry."

"But, why, Spencer? Why did you do it?" Kate wanted to know. There had to be explanations for all these weird and scary goings-on. Maybe alien possession wasn't such a strange idea.

"Yes, Spencer. What do you think you're playing at, swindling my brother?"

Kate cast a disbelieving glance Bridget's way. Like she'd ever supported her brother before, and certainly not against her fiancé! For some reason that Kate failed to detect, it was in Bridget's best interests to align herself with Tom rather than Spencer in the current situation.

Slowly Spencer turned to face Bridget. He grabbed one of her hands but she snatched it away from him. "I did it for you," he said.

Of all the things he could have said to kill Kate's sympathy for him stone dead that was it. Fancy swindling his best friend and business partner and then blaming someone else for it, like it wasn't anything to do with him.

"Oh, please. Whatever you've done it's nothing to do with me!" Bridget even moved her chair away as far as room would allow.

"You kept insisting on this holiday and that car, this piece of jewellery. Always more expensive than the last. Always changing the wedding plans; always more expensive schemes to make everyone jealous of you. Always more, more, more. You just see me as an everlastingly deep pocket don't you. Well, this is what it's come to."

"You can't blame me for that. All you had to do was say no."

"Oh, come on. You'd have run a mile if I ever tried to say no to you."

"I'd rather you'd refused me than that you swindled my brother."

"You're laying it on a bit thick, Bridge," Tom said.

Kate was forced to agree although not out loud. Bridget was indeed laying it on a bit thick.

"I am so sorry, Tom. Can you forgive me?" Spencer asked. "I wouldn't do it again. I'll show good faith in the first place by calling off the wedding. In fact, calling off the entire

105

engagement. It's costing too much and I think Bridget is just in it for what she can get."

Bridget shrieked. Not in a devastated way, but in an outraged, you'll-be-sorry way.

"That *is* my sister you're talking about, Spencer. So watch it. And, no, I don't think we can just forget it like it's never happened. How can I possibly trust you now?"

"But the whole point about confessing here and now is that we forgive each other."

"You didn't confess," Tom pointed out bluntly. "I had to do it for you even when you knew you'd been caught out. Even if you had, I don't know if I could forgive you. You relied on our lifelong friendship to swindle me. How could I ever trust you again?"

Poor Tom. In the space of an overloaded plate of tiramisu and a few squares of soft nougat, he'd lost his fiancée, his best friend and his business partner. It was almost enough for Kate to take him back. But not quite. She was way past sacrificing herself. Finally, she had realised that sane, well-balanced people didn't do that just for the sake of peace.

Chapter Thirteen

Had there ever been such a horrendous New Year's Day dinner confession time? No. There hadn't. Most people sat in their seats stunned and drained of response. Kate had a horrible feeling that there would never again be a Three Families Event – that their golden childhood had gone forever and no one would ever be happy again. On the other hand, maybe things had been *too* idyllic and it was time the real world got a look-in.

She glanced at Stella to see her still sitting at the head of the wrecked dinner table; her husband had brought a chair so he could sit next to his wife, his arm along her shoulders. This had to be the first time anyone had dared to rearrange the seating plan to that extent which just went to show how catastrophic things were.

Kate tried to imagine what her parents were seeing from the top of the table. They could see their disgraced son, suspended from the police force for apparently taking bribes from criminals. Kate doubted Stella would ever believe that to be true even if she actually witnessed the filthy lucre changing hands into her first-born's grubby palms.

Stella could also see Kate, her daughter who let the side down years ago by refusing to go to university, preferring instead to immerse herself in the world of growing things, and now, compounding the sin by breaking off her engagement to the perfectly good candidate who'd been by her side her whole life: Tom, in fact, appeared to be the only half decent person sitting at this table according to tonight's revelations.

"Well, I was going to say that I'd lost my licence from speeding and getting too many points, but it seems like such a let-down in comparison to other people's revelations that I hardly dare utter the words," Errol Hamilton said.

"Don't then!" Marilyn snapped.

Kate knew he'd been driving in the early hours of this morning. Did that mean he was driving illegally? Or was he attempting humour? It hardly seemed to matter now.

Errol kept going. "Also, in church I accidentally threw a two pound coin into the collection and made the chap stand there while I fished it out and replaced it with a pound. I did feel suitably ashamed of my meanness afterwards. Of course I can't say any of that now, either."

"You don't go to church," Kate said. She decided he must be trying to lighten the mood. He wasn't doing a very good job of it!

Their traditional coffee, confections and confession time wasn't built for the magnitude of revelations it'd had to deal with this year. It was like expecting a cage constructed to house a budgie to keep an eagle in comfort.

In fact, it was a complete shambles. People started clumping together around the table, collecting in clearly drawn up islands of solidarity. Pete Benning and Marilyn Hamilton. Spencer Hamilton with his dad – Kate couldn't tell who was more inebriated now between those two. Bridget sat alone stabbing at a piece of soft nougat on her plate. Stella and Dad Benning still sat at the head of the table – they appeared to be leaning on each other. Kate was alone but she had Jeff-Dog so she didn't feel alone. Although he sat next to her, Tom was by himself. Clark and his half-brother Errol Hamilton muttered together. Kate couldn't see Mum Cole at all. Maybe she'd hidden herself in one of the bedrooms to lick her wounds. Dad Cole conferred in undertones with Mum Hamilton.

They all needed a Zorro to turn up, cape flowing, that particular sort of hat square on his head, sword flashing to cut away the crap and leave a New Year standing clean and ready for living. But there wasn't a Zorro for everyone. Just for her.

She barely stopped herself grinning. It didn't seem appropriate. But it was peculiarly exciting and comforting to know there was a hero keeping an eye on her at all times – ready to protect her and to steal a dog for her.

Tom gave her a strange look and she wondered if she'd managed to subdue her grin as much as she thought she had. To cover herself she stood up and started to clear the table, stacking plates and discarding uneaten confections.

They would always remember this New Year's Day dinner. It would be forever seared upon their brains. Just as well she'd managed to get in her broken engagement before this latest crop of revelations. She simply couldn't have added it to everything else that had happened; it seemed tame in comparison now.

She trudged out to the kitchen, offloaded the dirty crockery into a sink full of soapy water, and trudged back to the dining room for more. Jeff-Dog followed her all the way.

Even taking receipt of a stolen dog from a masked bandit and disguising him with Bridget's hair dye plus a knitted balaclava seemed like the stuff of a wholesome adventure, and no longer the law-breaking devilment she'd felt it was just a few hours ago.

Stella had joined her and attacked the washing up as though it were her personal enemy. Kate collected a fresh, warm tea-towel from the Aga and started drying the plates, quietly placing them one at a time in the cupboard. The wet sudsy plates and bowls just kept coming and she was pleased to have such a mundane chore to concentrate on, a chore she usually would have tried to avoid. Carefully making sure not to leave any streaks she dried another plate and put it in the sideboard. They all had their place and she was careful to get the right plates in the right place.

One day her mother would submit to getting a dishwasher. Instead of seeing it as an invention of the devil maybe she'd start to see it as merely a convenient way of getting used dishes from the table back into the sideboard where they lived instead of all this palaver with bubbly water, getting your hands all messed up, needing gallons of hand cream to put them right again, and then wiping germs all over the plates with a cloth.

"Pete can't be a corrupt policeman," she said, concentrating hard on spreading as many germs as possible onto a gravy dish. "Can he?"

"Of course not!" her mother snapped, energetically enough to throw soapy water around the place. "It's lies. All of it."

"But he's been suspended."

"That doesn't mean he's done it. '*Suspended pending enquiry*', remember. It doesn't mean he's done it. It means they're going to investigate. And when they do investigate they'll find he didn't do it. They'd better make their apology a good one, too, or I'll have something to say about it! In the local press if necessary!"

"He's saying he's going to leave the force, anyway."

"We won't let him. It will make him look bad if he does that."

"I don't think you can stop him if that's what he wants to do."

"It'll only be because he doesn't want to work for an organisation that hasn't shown any faith in him by suspending him."

"Or because he's guilty and wants to get away," Kate said too quickly for thought. She wished she hadn't said it.

"If you can't show a bit more loyalty you can leave now!"

Kate agreed with her mother's sentiment but wasn't going to say so. "I just want to know what's going on. I wouldn't say this anywhere else but in here."

"I should hope not," Pete said. Kate jumped. She'd thought he was too involved with his pregnant lover to approach the kitchen. "Comes to something when your own sister can't even back you up."

"What? Like you've backed me up all my life?" she said, surreptitiously moving away from him. You could never be too certain how he was going to react.

"I've always been there if you needed me."

"Give me an example." She'd hit the fridge now and couldn't back off any further, but she wasn't going to let him get away with this bullshit. While she'd been envying friends their brothers, hers had been her worst bully.

He gave her such a look that she felt almost afraid, but he said nothing, so she gave an example: "Oh, I know, what about the time when Zit Henderson stole my new bike and wouldn't let me have it back? He stood there, just down the lane, leaning on my bike and yelling insults at me. '*Tree trunk*' was one of them, and '*thick legs, thick head*'. I've never been happy in a skirt since. What about then?"

"What about then?" he snapped.

"I was crying and screaming and trying to think of horrible things to yell back – and failing – and every time I got close to my bike he'd just push me away and I'd fall over. And then you turned up. My big brother to the rescue. I'd never been so pleased to see anyone in my life before." Kate stared at Pete and he stared right back, no flicker of shame in his stance at all, which made her even crosser.

"What did he do?" Stella asked. "I remember that. I remember you coming home with your hands and your knees all grazed. You said someone had taken your bike and you'd fallen over trying to chase him." Stella looked at Kate, her eyebrows raised in query. "But you had your bike," she added.

Kate had forgotten her mother was in the kitchen with them to witness this. She felt bad for her now and hesitated, but Pete wasn't having it. "Get on with it then. What did I do?"

"You don't remember?" Somehow that infuriated Kate even more! "You did nothing! You left me to get on with it and walked off, whistling!"

"Pete?" Stella queried, turning to her first-born.

"I didn't do nothing. I did everything. I told you to get off your arse, quit whingeing and moaning and wringing your hands, and sort him out. It was Zit Henderson, ferchrissakes!"

"And then you walked off," Kate reminded him. "You just walked off and left me to it."

111

"Did you, Pete?" Stella demanded. "Did you just leave her to it?"

"I did walk off. To the nearest bush and then I hid in it to make sure she was okay. And so I was in prime position to see her forget her need to uselessly grizzle. She beat him to a pulp and got her bike back."

"Kate!" Stella exclaimed. "You beat him to a pulp?"

Oh, how quickly the victim becomes the bully when the victim gets the upper hand! The irony of it was not lost on Kate even in the middle of her current confusion. She'd had no idea that Pete stayed to make sure she was okay. She stared at him, seeing the whole incident play out in her mind's eye in a completely different light to the one she was used to viewing it in. She didn't know what to say.

"I didn't bring you up to '*beat people to a pulp*'!" her mother said.

"Zit Henderson deserved it," Pete said in a tone of voice so final his mother could find nothing to say.

"I'm getting used to skulking in bushes on your behalf," Pete said cryptically, staring back at Kate as if she'd get the message. But she was at a loss as to what he meant. "Especially rhododendron bushes," he added, and she had a sudden flash back to being in the garden earlier that night and hearing a commotion in the bushes and thinking it was Zorro. It wasn't Zorro? It was Pete keeping an eye on her? She tried to ignore the idea. She'd hate to think she'd been lusting after Zorro when it turned out to be her brother...

"And yes, I heard Tom being all maudlin about his parents," Pete said. "I don't know who is lying the hardest – Tom about his concern for his parents, or his parents about their apparent rift, or Mum Hamilton and Dad Cole about their apparent affair."

"You don't think any of it is true?" Kate said. Why would Tom have put on such an act if none of it were true?

"Do you really think it's true?" Pete asked her.

Kate didn't know what to think any more. The desire to go home and go to bed was overwhelming.

The desire to have her Zorro come galloping in, whisk her up in to his arms and ride off into the sunset was also overwhelming. As long as it was *her* Zorro…

And Jeff-Dog, who'd been ardently licking the floor, leapt to his feet and galloped across the kitchen to her like an arrow speeding to the heart of its target. And everything was all right again, regardless of other people and the games they played.

Without saying more, Pete left the kitchen.

Kate smiled at her mother whose comments on recent revelations were conspicuous by their absence, and left the kitchen, too. Closely followed by her faithful hound.

Out in the hall Kate checked no one was around before tiptoeing its length to the alcove near the front door. She had to pass a few doors on the way but was certain no one had spotted her. Once at her destination she had another look around. No, no one was there. She dived behind the coats and landed with a 'thunk' on the padded shelf that had been her hidey hole forever.

Everyone pretended they didn't know it was there. It was hers. And now it was hers and Jeff-Dog's. He jumped up and wedged himself alongside her, one paw jammed on her thigh to keep himself upright. It was as if he'd been doing it his whole life. The alcove 'ceiling' curved into an arch so they both tilted their heads towards the middle of the space to save themselves concussion. It was comforting being cheek by jowl with her furry friend in the dark while she tried to sort out her thoughts.

Not that she wanted to think about her thoughts at all. They were too upsetting, most of them. She would have liked to think about her Zorro but then again the thought that she might have confused her Zorro with her brother was too awful to contemplate. So, instead, she thought back to previous times when she'd been in her hidey hole. Her family would stand outside the camouflaging coats, jackets and scarves hung on the pegs, plus the odd hat, and they'd muse out loud, apparently without knowing she was in there.

113

Like the time when she'd made such a fool of herself in the school play. She'd been a crow in the nativity. A crow. She barely kept back a snort of laughter now. She flung her arm around Jeff-Dog and grinned into his fur. She'd been a crow... But she'd been a very unfortunate crow...

As she'd been waiting for her cue to trip crow-like on to the stage and deliver her few lines of cawing she'd sat down to have a read of the book she always had on her. In that case it had been about a little white horse since when she'd had a love for salmon pink geraniums almost as great as her love for fuchsias.

Thinking of which – she hadn't read it for a while. It was time for another outing. She felt around underneath the seat and sure enough found several books under there. Without seeing them she knew there'd also be one about the little grey men and another one about a little wooden horse. It was nice to think her old favourites would forever be there for her.

She'd always had a book on her even when she'd been told she mustn't shove one in her waistband or under her shirt. When she was a crow and she sat down to read whilst waiting to go on-stage, she'd knocked over an incautiously abandoned beaker of orange squash and sat in a puddle of juice while she read, unaware upon jumping up in answer to her cue, that her tail feathers had disintegrated so completely her knickers were revealed to the world. This wouldn't have been so bad if she'd been wearing her usual voluminous dark green knickers but she'd been wearing her special knickers – the ones she wore when she wanted more courage than she felt she had by herself. Emblazoned on the back of these bright yellow knickers were the words: "I CAN do it."

Pete had given them to her she remembered now with a jolt of revelation. Maybe her brother *had* always been there for her but she hadn't recognised it.

When she came off stage Pete had been waiting for her with his jumper which he tied around her waist by its arms. He hadn't said a word and neither had anyone else while he'd been there. Afterwards plenty of her so-called friends had delighted in telling her that her knickers had been on show. Even now, people who'd been there, and some who hadn't but who had heard of it, would say things like "CAN I do it? Oh, yes I CAN do it..." and she'd had to learn to ignore it as if it meant absolutely nothing, but she was always suspicious when anyone, even complete strangers, used a phrase similar to that one.

She'd spent a lot of time in her hidey-hole after that and quite often there would be conversations on the other side of the coats that went like this:

Her dad would say: "Any idea where Kate is?"

Her mum would say: "Nope. She's probably in the tree house."

Her dad: "Do you think she's over the crow business?"

Her mum: "Oh, yes. Of course. She's a bright child. She'll have realised by now that people are only unkind about things like that because they CAN'T do what she can."

Dad: "Do you think so? Do you think she realises how clever she really is?"

Mum: "Oh, yes. She's bright enough to know she's bright."

And Kate would feel a warm glow come over her and she'd know that she really could do anything she chose to regardless of what anyone said, or what it said on her knickers.

And then Pete would come along and say: "She should think herself lucky she had any knickers on at all. Imagine if they'd disintegrated in that orange juice as well as her crow's tail. Not to mention she should be thankful they were yellow so it didn't look like she'd peed herself."

That gave her nightmares but it did make her think that yes, she was lucky she'd had any knickers on at all regardless of what was printed on them. And she was glad they were yellow, too...

Many of the upsets in her life had been sorted out while she'd been hidden in her cubbyhole and her family

115

pretended she couldn't hear them on the other side of the coats.

She had a great family! And she was going to be more appreciative of them in future, too. Oh, yes!

Chapter Fourteen

What a shame it was, this shambles of a dinner, what a waste of years of friendship. Kate wondered if there would ever be another Three Families New Year's Day Dinner again? Another confections and confessions session? Somehow she doubted it. Sadness enveloped her. It was like her life until now had been a sham.

Then her dad, who was magic and always knew what she was feeling, was there on the other side of the coats, speaking to her in a low voice: "No, my sweet Kate. You did have an idyllic childhood. Nothing can ever change that. You can't look back and overlay the golden years with new knowledge. That is being unfair to everyone. There is no reason why life can't be just as good again, in a different way. I'm sorry about your break-up with Tom. I'm sorry if it hurt you, although the way you did it felt a tad on the perfunctory side, an opportunistic break up, if you will."

Kate stuck her head out through the coats so she could see him, although that wasn't easy in the gloom of the hall. "You're right. I broke it off with him three months ago." She was too weary to keep up the pretence and she knew nothing went any further than her dad whatever she said to him. "He didn't want me to tell anyone. I think he thought we'd get back together again."

"Ah, well. He has my sympathy. It would be hard to lose you. However, it is still a New Year. There is no telling where we can go from here, what new avenues will open up, new adventures to pursue."

She smiled hopefully. Something she'd just been thinking she might never do again. "You're so great, Dad." She stood up and flung her arms around him and they hugged; Jeff-Dog stuck his nose in the back of her knee to contribute his bit of comfort to the occasion.

"I'll get on with the clearing up," Kate said. "At least it's something I can do without getting into too much trouble. How's Mum? She must be taking the news about Pete hard."

Her father's face stiffened. "Hmmm. About that. Had you got any inkling of this before?"

"No. Not at all. It came as a complete shock. I would never have believed it if I'd heard it anywhere else."

"You believe it because it was here you heard it?" He eyed her closely.

"Yes. Why would I not? Why would any of us lie to any of the rest of us?"

"What happened to innocent until proven guilty?"

Kate felt rather than saw her father withdraw from her a little. "I... Um... I don't know," she said. "You're right. I don't know why I believed it without question. I don't know why any of us would lie, though."

"Could you leave the dishes for a bit and go and see Mum Cole for me, please?" He wasn't going to cover up the change of topic at all. Kate nodded dumbly, feeling told off somehow. "She needs someone to show they care and I don't think I'm a suitable person," her dad continued. "But you are. She's fond of you. And take Jeff-Dog. He's a very comforting dog. She's at the top of the house in the back bedroom."

Dad Benning walked off and Kate remained still, trying to work out how she felt. Were they – and who were 'they' exactly? – lying about Pete? Why would they do that? She and Pete had never been very close. Maybe that was why she hadn't immediately declared his innocence. Not that he'd needed anyone else doing that. Stella had done it so ferociously that anyone would think Pete guilty no matter how innocent he might be.

Kate sighed and headed for the stairs. Jeff-Dog followed her as though they were attached to each other. Just thinking that made her feel better. Another living creature trusted her without question.

She didn't bother with lights having lived her whole life in this house until just a couple of years ago; she knew every corner and crevice of it. Climbing the flights of stairs brought memories back and she realised her dad was right. No matter what happened after it, her childhood had been bliss. She and the rest of The Three Families children could have been models illustrating all those stories about going on adventures with a scruffy dog, lashings of ginger beer and marmalade sandwiches.

Something made her stop. She listened hard. There had been a noise; she was sure of it. Bending down slowly to grab Jeff-Dog's collar she couldn't feel him within reach. Maybe it was him she'd heard. Straining her ears to listen even harder, she definitely heard something although the heavy pounding of blood through her veins was drowning it out. There was someone there but whoever it was couldn't be an axe-wielding murderer given the rapturous, snuffly greeting he or she was getting from Jeff-Dog.

"Who's there?" she whispered. She didn't know why she was whispering. Maybe because it was dark.

"It's me," someone whispered in reply and Kate's stomach, despite its heavy dinner-load, dissolved into nothingness. It was Zorro! Her fantasies about him had manifested him. She'd have to watch what she thought about in future.

"Oh," she exhaled on a breath. "Er. Hi."

By this time, a hazy figure, blacker than the rest of the blackness, had detached itself from the gloom and now stood in front of her, Jeff-Dog at his feet although she could only tell that because of the startlingly white ruff of fur Jeff-Dog had around his neck. What now? Her hero stood a mere breath away from her and she didn't know what to do.

"How are you doing?" he asked her, his voice so low she had to strain to catch it.

"I'm fine," she said softly. The very foundations of her life were crumbling beneath her feet but she didn't want her hero to think she was a wimp. She couldn't help but add: "It's been a strange evening, though. What about you? What have you been doing tonight? Saving people, galloping around on your horse, making it rear so you're a silhouette in the moonlight, your cape flying out behind you?"

"Horse? Um... cape?"

It was just as well it was dark on this landing or Zorro would see she must have suddenly become the colour of old radishes. "Er. You know. Like Zorro with his funny hat – wish I knew what it was called – or like Robin Hood, except he didn't ride a horse did he?"

"Sombrero Cordobés is the name of the hat I think you mean. As far as Robin Hood on a horse is concerned, I think Kevin Costner might have ridden a horse, but I'm not sure if previous Robin Hoods did."

Ooh, he liked movies. That had to be a good sign. She liked movies too. "And then there's that other chap – um – Scarlet Pimpernel. Riding around and killing off baddies with his sword."

"I could manage a motorbike. Is that any good? I'm not sure about a sword, though..."

"And Zorro wears a black silk mask."

"Ah, well. My balaclava is pure lamb's wool. Hope that's okay."

"And he swings in and rescues people."

"Do you need rescuing?"

She sighed. "Tonight's been the sort of night that I wish I'd been rescued from before it happened. Now that it has happened it's a bit late to be rescued. It's changed things forever." Despite her own Zorro standing right there, sadness threatened to envelop her.

"That's not necessarily a bad thing. Sometimes things need to change before people realise that a different path could be better for them than the well-trodden one."

"I can't see how any of tonight will turn out to be good, but I'm willing to give it a chance."

"This bit of tonight is good," he murmured, finger under her chin, tilting her face up. His lips brushed hers and she felt life surge back into her with a zing long forgotten. Things were looking up already. She couldn't bring herself to worry about the fact that she was kissing a strange man in her parents' house. Someone she had no idea who it was, or what he was involved in, or how he came to be associated with anything to do with any of The Three Families, or even how he was here at all.

No matter what he turned out to be, the thought of him over the last twenty-four hours had helped carry her through. She had been bolstered by knowing that a man existed on the same planet as her who watched over her and was ready to step in should the need arise. And now she thrilled to his kiss which reached all the way through her, right down to her feet. She'd worry about the weirdness of it later.

And then he was gone and she collapsed against the wall, clutching onto a door frame until strength seeped back into her legs and her heart calmed down enough for her to hear other noises in the night.

Pulling herself upright she headed for the soft sounds of weeping.

Chapter Fifteen

Opening the door into the back bedroom she could make out the shape of Tom's mother lying on the bed. Moonlight showed up silvery tears until Mum Cole realised she was no longer alone, and covered her face with her hands. Jeff-Dog didn't hesitate. None of this worrying about whether he was intruding on someone, or did they really want his sympathy? No – he bounded on to the bed and threw himself full length beside Kate's ex-nearly-mother-in-law's prone body. She brought her arms up and hugged him to her. He hugged her back, or so it seemed to Kate. She sat in a chair in Mum Cole's line of sight by the bed and waited.

Time was difficult to monitor sitting there in the dark with the rest of the world going on outside. Dimly Kate could hear fireworks and occasional bursts of merriment drifting to her from the neighbourhood. Some people were starting their New Year in a party spirit even if that wasn't the prevailing mood in this house.

The Three Families New Year had got off to a somewhat rocky beginning, but what if Zorro was right? What if great changes were needed to make sure the future went smoothly? She felt certain there was a little gleam of wisdom to cling onto in that thought.

Mum Cole sat up in the gloom and leaned back against the headboard, Jeff-Dog still pressed firmly to her side, his head under her chin like a child.

"You know Clark is his, don't you?" she said by way of greeting.

"Uh," Kate choked, completely thrown by the unexpectedness of the statement. Did Mum Cole mean that Clark Hamilton was Dad Cole's son? By Mum Hamilton?

"Clark?" she said hesitantly. "He's Dad Cole's son? But I thought he was..."

"From a previous, tragically terminated relationship which no one dared ask about. Yes, I know. That's what we're all supposed to think. But he was the result of a liaison between my husband and Mum Hamilton all those years ago before any of the rest of you children came into being; even before the Hamiltons came to live around here. So everyone has always believed Mum Hamilton had a previous husband or fiancé who died. I always knew better, but I don't think anyone knew I knew. I don't know what Dad Hamilton thought about it all. I've always tended to avoid both Hamiltons so that I could avoid the truth of it."

"I can't work out the timings," Kate said. "Do you mean you and Dad Cole were already married at the time?"

"Married and expecting Tom."

"And you never said anything to him?"

"No. I wanted my marriage to work and as long as he didn't rub it in my face or leave my child fatherless, I was prepared to overlook some weakness of the flesh. As it were. I could never be entirely fair with Clark, though. I regret that. It wasn't his fault," Mum Cole said, feverishly stroking Jeff-Dog, much to his delight.

"But what on earth does Dad Cole see in her? She can't even make proper ice lollies. Not like you could. Hers tasted stale and always fell off the stick too early."

"Goodness. Is this my claim to fame? A particular flair for ice-lolly making?"

"No! But it's strange what you remember from childhood and Mum Hamilton never struck me as being much of a motherly sort of person despite the fact that she had three of her own and, uh, another one... Oh. Well. Sorry. Strictly speaking, four of her own."

"Don't tell anyone, will you?"

"No. Don't worry. I won't." Kate hastened to assure her of her discretion.

"I don't know what to do now. And my devoted husband is so far gone he hasn't even bothered to come and see if I'm okay. In fact, no one has but you and your lovely dog." She gave Jeff-Dog an extra hard hug and he wagged his tail enthusiastically in encouragement. Kate knew he was saying, '*more, more, gimme more hugs!*'

"Well, it's difficult to know what's best. I suppose you could try thinking what *you* want out of the situation?" Kate felt out of her depth, but had learnt recently that you needed to think about what you wanted and not let that be forgotten in the chaos of everyone else's requirements of you.

"What do you mean? They've declared themselves and that's that," Mum Cole said. "I just have to accept it."

"You don't have to accept anything you don't want to. No one does." Kate said, wondering vaguely why she'd never fully realised this herself before now.

"I think I want to keep him."

"Why would you want to do that?"

"I love him."

"How do you know? How can you be sure?" How *do* you know if you really, really love someone or if it's just infatuation or lust?

"I need to think about this a bit. I need to make sure it's not just a habit I've got in to – being married to him, I mean." Mum Cole peered at Kate. "What about you? What about you breaking off with my son? Poor Tom. Did you suddenly realise you weren't in love with him? How can you be so sure you've done the right thing?"

Because I've fallen in love with Zorro. Kate tried to think of something sensible to say but was too shaken by her own thoughts. She was in love with Zorro? How could she be? She didn't even know who he was.

"I'm not completely sure I *have* done the right thing," she said slowly as though the words had difficulty exiting her mouth. "My whole life I've known I'd end up with Tom. But maybe that's not a good way to be with someone. Just the idea of 'ending up' with someone? Nah. Sounds like something that happens if you're the last packet of biscuits on the shelf. You will end up being dunked in someone's tea because you're too stale to taste nice all by yourself. Anyway, I didn't like how possessive he got. Always wanting to know what I was doing and when and who with."

She glanced at what she could see of Mum Cole. "I'm sorry. This is your son I'm talking about."

"Don't be sorry. I could see he was stifling you. I did warn him. Under all that good-girl facade you have going for you, you're quite the little rebel really. I know your mother could never understand you not going to study law and taking up fuchsia-growing instead. She could never get her head around it and didn't realise her nagging you was as useless as trying to fence the wind. I did wonder about Tom, too, what he thought about it when it was what we'd all expected all along for you, but I thought he could cope with it. Maybe I was wrong. Maybe he's not as flexible-minded as I thought. I love him dearly, which means, contrary to popular belief, that I see him clearly. Ooh, that rhymes."

Kate wondered if Mum Cole had finally lost the plot. She'd never been what might be called fanciful, and yet here she was hugging a dog and making up rhyming couplets about what love meant. As for all that 'fence the wind' and 'good-girl façade' stuff – what was that about? It was weird to think of herself as the person Mum Cole was talking about.

"To get back to what I want," Mum Cole said. "I think I do want to keep my marriage."

"How can you make it work if Dad Cole has been having a fling – well – more than a fling – with Mum Hamilton for such a long time?"

"There was a big gap in the middle between the first fling and the current one."

"Even so, if they're picking up where they left off, it sounds a bit serious to me." Kate was suddenly afraid she'd overstepped the mark. It was difficult to forget she was speaking to one of the parents rather than someone at her own 'level' in The Three Families hierarchy.

"I think it might be my fault. I stopped trying some time ago. When Bridget left home, I think. Suddenly I couldn't see the point of anything and rather than turning to him, I turned within. If he knew I needed him he might come back to me. Maybe *he* needed *me*. Maybe Bridget leaving home changed him, too. How would I know? I've never asked him. This isn't just a one-sided thing. It takes two. It always takes two to tango."

Kate was impressed by Mum Cole's take on the situation and wondered if she could be that analytical about breaking up with Tom. Had she somehow made Tom over-possessive of her? She'd give it some thought later...

"I have noticed how neither of my own children have come to see if I'm all right," Mum Cole said. "Thank you for coming, Kate. I would have liked you for a daughter-in-law but one of the main advantages of this arrangement The Three Families have is that we get to share all our children so I sort-of have you anyway. If you don't mind."

"I don't mind at all. That's why you're all 'Mum' and 'Dad' to all of us. It's always been like one big, happy family. Not so happy now though."

"All families go through rough patches. Of course they do. This is just another rough patch. It's just that we've outdone ourselves this time."

"So, what are you going to do about Dad Cole?"

"I'm going to get him back. But somehow I need to do it so it puts a dent in *his* complacency, too."

"How? Him and Mum Hamilton seemed keen on getting it together again."

"I haven't told him that I need him and love him. I can't remember the last time I did that. If he still wants her then that's that, but I would regret it forever if I didn't try to tell him. As for her, I'm going to give her a smack. That lazy cow could have had anyone. She's like that. Men are attracted to her like flies to a rotting hog."

Kate flinched at the mental juxtaposition she'd been given of Mum Hamilton and a decaying pig corpse blurred by

126

millions of buzzing iridescent flies. She could almost smell it and started to breathe through her mouth.

"She could have had anyone," Mum Hamilton went on. "Why would she take a man from The Three Families? She deserves a slap. And she's getting one."

"I thought you always said that violence never solved anything. I can't imagine you doing it either."

"Violence *doesn't* solve anything. But in this case it'll make me feel better. The other thing I'll be aiming for – apart from her face – is the shock that it'll give Dad Cole. It'll be the last thing he expects me to do. He'll be stunned and then I'll go in for the kill. Well, not the kill exactly. I don't want him, or anyone, dead. But that's when I'll tell him that I love him and need him and that he has to stay with me. He'll see me in a whole new light and our love can begin anew."

Kate wondered if Mum Cole was under the influence of something seriously toxic. She fumbled through the dark and lightly placed her hand on the afflicted woman's brow. No, it was cool, not at all feverish. "When were you thinking of attacking Mum Hamilton?" she asked. "I would like to see this." Kate didn't really believe Mum Cole would do it, but if it was going to happen, and she had prior knowledge of it, she would so totally kick herself if she missed it. Not that she'd ever had anything in particular against Mum Hamilton before, or anything *for* her, come to that – but it was different now, and she was pulling for Mum Cole whatever she decided to do.

Mum Cole swung her legs to the side of the bed and stood up, Jeff-Dog sliding off her and flopping onto the pillows. Kate said, "Oy! Off the bed, you!" He scrabbled onto the floor and stood next to her slowly waving his tail, a little smile on his furry face.

"Right then," Mum Cole said, and switched on a bedside lamp, momentarily blinding them all. Staring into the dressing table mirror, she fiddled with her hair, refreshed her lipstick, and looked at Kate. "Thank you for coming up to me. It was kind of you. I've always liked you. You were the only one who made sure to thank me for the ice-lollies. I would find your sticks afterwards. They were the ones that had been unrolled. Some of them had pictures you'd drawn on them. I kept those."

Kate flushed, unable to look away from Mum Cole in the mirror. Good grief! She wondered if her own mother had kept her childish drawings. Somehow she doubted it. Anything regarded as non-essential got chucked out very quickly or taken to the nearest charity shop. "You ready?" she mumbled.

Chapter Sixteen

Their entrance in to the dining room caused a small lull in the conversations going on around the table, but not for long. Mum Cole stopped for a moment as though considering her course of action and then headed straight for Mum Hamilton. When she reached her, Mum Cole stood so close to her that although Mum Hamilton tried to ignore her, she couldn't. Not without looking like a complete idiot.

Dad Cole still sat next to Mum Hamilton. He looked up enquiringly at his wife, but Mum Cole was concentrating so totally on Mum Hamilton she didn't see his face. Kate could see it though, and she could clearly see that he still loved her. The expression on his face was unmistakeable. He yearned for his wife. He might as well have had it tattooed on his forehead.

So, why had he publicly humiliated his wife today, then, fer cryin' out loud, by declaring his affair in this way? What hold did Mum Hamilton have over him that he could make his affair with her so public even though he still loved his wife? The vision of a million flies hovering around a decaying hog came to mind but she hastily banished it. It made her feel itchy.

"Stand up," Mum Cole ordered Mum Hamilton. The latter's mouth fell open, and hers wasn't the only one. No one ever expected Mum Cole to order people about. Slowly Mum Hamilton stood up as though hypnotised by the commanding tone. As soon as she was upright, Mum Cole slapped her so hard the smacking sound echoed around the room. Jeff-Dog yelped and pressed himself into Kate's legs. This time, the lull in conversation was instant, absolute and sustained.

Except for Dad Cole, who leapt to his feet. "Bloody hell!" he shouted. "What are you doing?" he demanded of Mum Cole, and he shoved Mum Hamilton behind him as if to protect her from further attack.

Was that a hastily suppressed grin that flashed across his face Kate wondered, or was she imagining it?

"I love you," Mum Cole said to Dad Cole. "I need you, and I'm not taking this as an insuperable obstacle to our getting back together again. Oh... Well... As long as you haven't caught anything from her, of course."

"What?" Mum Hamilton squeaked, unsuccessfully trying to get past Dad Cole. He held her back at the same time as warding Mum Cole off.

"And you can dump her as soon as you like," Mum Cole said, making another lunge at her competition. "Or do you think you might in fact have caught something sordid from this sleazebag?"

Sleazebag??? Kate stowed that one away for when she might need it. Sleazebag!

Dad Cole easily kept the women apart. "Violence never solved anything, Gill," he said, a trifle stuffily, Kate thought. Blimey. A woman, usually fairly retiring, attacks another woman in such a way that it must inflate her husband's ego to the size of Australia, and he quotes her own saying back at her in an asking-for-it tone of voice. And expects to get away with it...

No chance.

"I know that!" Mum Cole shrieked and smacked Dad Cole as well. "That's for being a prig when you should have been a hero!" Then she turned to Dad Hamilton who'd been hovering on the edge of the gathering, and smacked him as well, although Kate fancied her slaps were beginning to lose power now. "And that's for being such a wimp. Get your wife in hand!"

Mum Cole then suddenly turned around and looked at the assembled crowd, not a few of whom cowered back, apparently wondering if they were going to be next. Kate nearly laughed but controlled herself in time. "I want coffee now and some of the soft nougat stuff. I missed it while I was breaking my heart upstairs where no one came to see if I was okay, until Kate did. Yes, I'll have coffee thank you. And then it'll be my turn for confessions."

Stella rushed forward and guided Mum Cole to her seat, poured her coffee, stirred in cream, handed her a bowl of the nougat and went back to her own place, a little smile on her face that puzzled Kate, unless it was because she was pleased to see her friend finally come out of her shell.

But, what did Mum Cole have to confess? Out of all of them she was the one who was never likely to do *anything* that required a confession. This was obviously the main thought in everyone's mind as they all came and sat down again at the table. A renewed round of coffee pouring and passing of confections took place. Even Mum Hamilton and Dad Cole joined in. Everyone flicked glances at each other. Uncertainty filled the air.

Mum Cole maintained silence until the whole room stilled. It was so quiet that when Jeff-Dog vigorously scratched himself, the sound filled the room like a waterfall breaking loose from its course and tearing through a dry cornfield. The sound was so very alive that Kate itched in response and furiously rubbed her own arm. Realising what she was doing, she leant over and stroked Jeff-Dog to distract herself, and him, from their scratching. She wondered if he needed defleaing – not something she was inclined to mention just now, though.

"Well," Stella said to the star of the moment. "Out with it. What's your confession?"

Mum Cole straightened in her chair and looked around at her audience. All eyes were on her. "My hanging baskets, which I won the village competition with, were bought already planted," she announced, casually taking a sip of her coffee. "I didn't plant them myself at all. I'm a fraud."

The collective indrawn breath must have been audible across the other side of the city. It was followed by a few choking coughs and one stray giggle.

131

"Not only that," she continued. "But I was the one who defaced the new tribute sculpture in the village. Let's face it – it's hideous. Someone had to do it. Fancy putting up such an awful commemoration to an artist and totally failing to do justice to his vision with a gargoyle-thing like that. I'm a vandal."

This was greeted with complete silence. Kate imagined everyone trying to visualise Mum Cole out in the night with spray paint, and failing.

And then she said: "No, I'm not. I'm just kidding. I didn't do either of those things. Fancy thinking I would!"

This caused even more consternation. Mum Cole had never been the kidding sort. It was unthinkable that she would say such things as a joke. It was unthinkable that she would ever lie in any way, no matter how small the fib might be. It was also doubtful that she even knew *how* to be a fraud, or a vandal.

"My confession is..." Everyone leant forward, all agog. "My confession is that I finally realise, in amongst all the affairs and the corruption that you lot seem to find commonplace that my infringements are, and always have been, entirely trivial to the rest of you. No wonder you laugh."

No one made a sound. Certainly no one laughed.

"So, I'm going to up my game. For a start I'm going to have an affair. It's about time."

Still there wasn't a sound. Kate found herself yearning for a marching band to forge its way through the room, or a rockfall to drown out the sound of there being no sound.

"Yep. I'm going to have an affair. I'm not yet sure with whom. I shall consider my options, but possibly with my husband once he's realised how silly he's being. He's not there yet. Evidently." This last was said with such a scathing look at Dad Cole where he sat with Mum Hamilton leaning on his shoulder that Kate was surprised flames didn't erupt out of the carpet.

132

Everyone turned to check out Dad Cole who pretended they weren't all staring at him, although a raspberry flush crept out from under his collar, stained his throat and climbed up to his face.

"My confession," Mum Cole continued, a look of some startlement on her own face as if she hadn't realised she was going to say what she was going to say: "is that I am taking over my daughter's role in the flower shop and I'm moving out of my marital home while she moves back into it. I will be working in the shop and living in the flat that goes with it. I'm not sure why it's a confession, really. It's not a bad thing. I wish I'd thought of it before. It's time I did something else with my life apart from being a wife and a mother."

Still no one spoke.

Mum Cole turned to her husband. "I know you're not really having an affair with Mum Hamilton, although you must have had such fun coming up with this scheme to make a fool of me in public. I know that within The Three Families we don't consider this to be public exactly, but I do. You have exposed me to ridicule and you might have been doing it to wake me up to the fact that I've neglected you since the children left home and that you might have suffered, too, since they went. Not to mention trying to wake up Dad Hamilton to some kind of similar realisation, but the way you chose to do it was appallingly insensitive. I love you and want our marriage to continue. But for that to happen you're going to have to start again with me if you want me. From tonight, you know where I live. Feel free to come a-courting."

"No, it's not like that, Gill…" Dad Cole started, but got no further. He looked down and Kate had the sense that he wanted to say something else but for some reason was unable to. Unexpectedly, she felt sorry for him.

"I'm not moving back home!" Bridget said, outrage sharpening her voice to an unappealing screech.

"Yes, you are," Mum Cole said. "You're just playing around at the floristry business. You're not paying your share

133

of the rent. You're expecting Spencer to foot all your bills. You need to move home again until you can afford to do what you want rather than expecting everyone else to pay for you. As it is, you'll be living off your father."

Kate checked out Dad Cole's expression. Yes, he looked horrified.

"Don't expect to get anything from what I earn with the florist's shop," Mum Cole continued. "This will be a whole new learning experience for me, too, and I don't want you dragging me down. After all, you *are* twenty-three! Poor Spencer. No wonder he buckled into embezzlement to keep you happy. Not that that's an excuse, but it makes it a little more understandable that he swindled his partner and best friend for the woman he loves. This way you'll have to look after your father in return for board and lodging. It's time you did something useful instead of swanning about as though someone else should look after you for the rest of your life."

Bridget was left speechless, her mouth opening and shutting soundlessly like a beached cod.

Mum Cole startled Kate by suddenly turning to her. For a moment she was afraid of what was coming her way. "The flats *are* entirely separate aren't they, Kate? I mean, it's not going to impinge on you, is it?"

"No. Not at all. It won't make any difference to me at all."

"Except that you know the rent will be paid on time," Mum Cole said flicking her daughter a knowing look. Bridget stared back, mutiny in every line of her body. Her mother smiled at her which made her pinch her lips even more tightly together, but she apparently still had nothing to say.

"Anyway, I'm going home now. I'm tired." Mum Cole strode over to her daughter. Even the way she walked had become out-of-character, and purposeful. She gestured at Bridget in an imperious manner. "Keys," she barked, and her daughter handed them over without a murmur, receiving in return the keys for her old, childhood home – the home she thought she'd left forever a few years ago. "And your car keys," Mum Cole demanded.

Bridget opened her mouth to argue but shut it again.

Surprisingly, Spencer Hamilton attempted to remonstrate. "Mum Cole, you're taking things too far."

Mum Cole stared at him as though he'd crawled out from under the skirting board. He flushed and looked away, but still mumbled loudly enough to be heard, "Bridget will still need her car…"

"Bridget will be going home with her father in his car. She won't need her car for a while."

"But, her car is a sports car…" Spencer said.

"So? I'm not so out of shape I can't get into it! Or is there an age limit to driving a sports car of which I'm unaware?" She stared at him and Kate knew that no one could come back from that glare, least of all Spencer, never known for his backbone anyway.

Sure enough, Spencer gave up, and slumped back with an audible groan of defeat. Mum Cole waved her hand at Bridget again and her daughter produced her car keys and sulkily dumped them into her mother's palm.

It was so weird to think of this particular woman making off to a new place without even a nightie or a toothbrush to her name. Everyone in the room remained silent. In the doorway Mum Cole turned to her husband. "You know where I'll be. You're going to have to earn the right to be with me again," she said. He gazed at her as though she were someone he'd never met in his life before. Which he probably hadn't. None of them had, Kate thought. Still. Change is as good as a rest. Right? You need change to move forward.

What about too much change though? Was there such a thing as too much change?

"Now I am completely confused," Marilyn Hamilton said. "Is Mum Cole really a secret graffiti artist?" She looked around, eyes wide.

"No, she's not a graffiti artist!" Dad Cole snapped.

"And what about her hanging baskets, then? She won the competition with them, and now she's saying she didn't plant them herself? That *is* fraud, you know."

135

"My wife is not a fraud!" Dad Cole yelled in a strangled voice as if pushed to the limit of his self-control.

Kate stifled a smile at the outrage in Dad Cole's tone. The very idea that being married to him for thirty years might have turned his wife to a life of rampant crime without him knowing was not sitting well with him.

"Well, is she having an affair with Dad Hamilton, then?" Marilyn persevered. "She's having an affair with someone. She said so."

"No, she's not!" Dad Cole yelled thumping the table in his fury, his face darkening in what Kate was afraid was a horribly unhealthy manner. It wouldn't do Mum Cole any good at all to have brought her husband to the realisation that she was still a woman and still needed his attention, only to have him keel over with a heart attack. Kate passed him a glass of water, which he glanced at but ignored. "She is not having an affair with anyone," he ground out.

"Well, I think it's all very strange," Marilyn continued somewhat ponderously. "Mum Cole never lies. She's the only one of us who never lies. So, who's she having an affair with then?"

"Me!" Dad Cole snapped.

"Well, that's silly. You're her husband. She can't have an affair with you. Can she?"

Before Dad Cole attempted to answer this one, Stella Benning said, "And what do you mean, Marilyn, by saying she's the only one of us who never lies? That's what I want to know."

Marilyn had nothing to say to this and lowered her head submissively. No one in their right mind deliberately got on the wrong side of Stella Benning.

"What on earth does 'come a-courting' mean?" Bridget asked into the silence, earning herself a look of complete contempt from her father. Kate wondered how they were going to get on living together again without the buffer that Mum Cole had always been.

Bridget didn't really have to go back to her childhood home, but given that she seemed incapable of looking after

136

herself financially speaking – or was too lazy to attempt it – she probably would. Maybe Dad Cole would move out in defeat and Bridget would end up in sole possession of the family home. That probably would happen to Bridget. She always landed on her feet, that one. Kate felt a grudging admiration for such self-obsession and ability to survive regardless of the current crisis.

More coffee was poured, liqueurs sampled, confections pushed around plates as The Three Families, somewhat stunned and minus one of their founding parents, mulled over the events of this New Year's Day.

Chapter Seventeen

Kate settled back in her chair but couldn't relax. Her brain kept running around in her skull like a rat lost in a maze. The evening had been too disturbing. Her life as she'd known it until now seemed to be unravelling in front of her eyes and she was unable to do anything about it.

She was discovering all kinds of advantages to having a dog, too. He could be used for many and varied excuses.

"I've just got to take Jeff-Dog out," she said, standing up and heading for the kitchen and back door.

"That dog must have a weak bladder!"

Kate ignored the comment and carried on through to the garden, Jeff-Dog trotting beside her, happily unaware aspersions had been cast on his holding ability.

Once his paws hit the springiness of the lawn, Jeff-Dog bounced around, ecstatic with the nectar of freedom. It was infectious and Kate couldn't help but race after him. He thought this was a great game and ran even further. She tried to keep up but pretty soon was puffing and wheezing. She stopped to lean over, her hands on her knees. She was so unfit! The trees seemed to whisper agreement.

Looking up, she couldn't see Jeff-Dog in the darkness. She tried to call him back but her breathless yells of "Jeff-Dog!" came out as squeaks which didn't carry on the breeze. Even if they had, there was some doubt that he would recognise his name, having only had it for such a short while, and even if she had enough breath, she couldn't yell "Rover" or everyone would know he was the Stolen Dog from the Badlands.

As the wind shifted clouds around, bands of light came and went across the lawn, sometimes revealing the shrubs and trees around the edge of the property, sometimes throwing them into an impenetrable darkness cutting off The Three Families New Year's Day gathering from the rest of the world.

In a moonlit moment Kate spotted Jeff-Dog. She also spotted someone – was it Zorro? For a moment her breathlessness returned – until she realized the figure was leaning over that poor, unsuspecting pooch as though to clip a lead on to his collar. Then they ran off, Jeff-Dog's excited yips clearly encouraging whoever it was to run faster.

He thought everything was a game, that dog! Even when he was being stolen! When she got him back she was having words with him. Serious words about never trusting people. Well – unless it was *her* doing the stealing…

Already out of breath, she forced her body to move faster but nothing she could do made any difference and she fell further and further behind as her innocent, love-everyone dog was taken from her. Who could she call about a double-stolen dog? She could just imagine what the police would say.

What about Pete? He might be suspended, but surely his mates on the force would know he was innocent and he could get them to help. But then, she might be putting him in more trouble. Jeff-Dog was already stolen after all. Tears flooded down her face and she hiccupped a few times, her mind blank with terror. Who would just run off with her dog like that? She didn't know what to do. Where was Zorro when she really needed him?

She reached into her pocket for her mobile phone thinking she'd ring Tom. She'd always gone to him when in trouble and he might know what to do. But she stopped when a dark figure raced past her. Zorro! He hadn't let her down. What a hero!

"Stay there. I'll get him…" His words floated back to her as he disappeared into the night. Kate waited for her heart to stop making such a racket and then she listened hard. The sounds of pursuit through dense undergrowth could easily be heard, the crashing of feet onto frosted leaves and fallen twigs, the eager yelps of a dog enjoying this new game to the full.

Then it went quiet and Kate stopped breathing in case she missed hearing some telling sound, and jumped at a sudden explosion of noise, presumably the sounds of a tussle.

Oh, how she hoped Zorro won! But of course he would win. He was Zorro.

And sure enough, before long Jeff-Dog's white ruff could be seen moving erratically through the gloom alongside a denser bit of night. They approached her at a run and Jeff-Dog hurled himself at her, impatient to tell her his adventures.

Zorro curled one of Kate's hands into one of his, and led her to the house. At the back door, he said, "Go inside. Please go inside and stay there. It's not safe for you or your dog to be alone at the moment." He leant forward and she couldn't help herself from meeting him halfway, but he merely kissed her cheek, and before she could query his odd assertion about their safety he was gone.

Did he mean not safe for her and him to be alone? As in he couldn't trust himself around her? Or her around him? The thought made her extraordinarily warm.

But surely he wouldn't then include Jeff-Dog?

It was a mystery – as was also the fact that her dog no longer wore his firework balaclava. She'd been up all night knitting that and someone had nicked it! So much for his disguise. Or maybe his balaclava had been removed to confirm to the dognapper that he was indeed Rover from the Badlands. She'd probably find it lying around where he'd chucked it after making sure he had the right dog, but she couldn't go and look for it now after Zorro saying she and Jeff-Dog should lie low for a while. She hesitated, but feeling even more confused than usual, she headed back inside for another round of soft nougat, taking her unmasked dog with her.

Jeff-Dog immediately took up position under the table as if he'd been doing it all his life, and Kate settled back into her seat, helped herself to more coffee and looked around.

Four of the younger generation Three Families men were missing. Pete was still there morosely and minutely examining the table cloth as though it had the answer to life's vexed questions. The others must have left the room soon after she did, as if her going outside with Jeff-Dog had signalled some sort of comfort break.

Idly, she wondered if any of them were Zorro, but she knew they couldn't be. Kate had known them all her life and she knew for a fact none of them were hero material. Oh, well, except maybe for Clark…

Or maybe they could all be if she thought about them differently…

Errol entered the room somewhat furtively. Kate noticed his lip looked split. Had he been thumped? The thought that he might have been the one to attempt the theft of Jeff-Dog theft made her wince. Surely not Errol. Her friend. But then, on further reflection, maybe he was Zorro – there was no saying that when Zorro rescued Jeff-Dog he hadn't been thumped himself. Was she imagining it or did he flush when he caught her eye? Hastily she looked down. She didn't know whether to look at Errol admiringly or with bared teeth. Was he a goodie or a baddie?

She looked up again and couldn't help herself from miming at her own lip and looking a question at him.

He laughed. "Stupid! I slipped on the patio slabs. They're quite slippery at the moment – the night is quite damp and very cold. Fell over and smacked my lip on one of the benches."

Kate gave a little acknowledging laugh in return but now she didn't know if he was Zorro, a dog stealer, a liar, or just a clumsy sod.

Clark and the others appeared and they all took their seats. Clark was out of breath and his hair was messy, but so was everyone else's, so it could have been the wind rather than chasing through the undergrowth that had done it. And maybe half of them were out of breath because they'd been out for a sly smoke. She'd lost track of who smoked and who didn't these days although she knew for sure that Tom didn't. She didn't think Zorro did either. She'd have smelt it on him.

If only she could think of a good reason she'd get up and try to get a whiff of Clark, Errol and Spencer to see if she could eliminate them from her Zorro-enquiries, but she couldn't think of a good reason to approach them sniffing wildly. That wouldn't look at all odd, would it?

Stumped, she filled her mouth with yet more nougat.

Chapter Eighteen

"She's been kidnapped!" Spencer announced, jumping to his feet and staring at his mobile phone. "Oh my God! It's Bridget. She's been kidnapped!" His voice rose and ended on an odd squeak.

He stared at Bridget.

"Don't be silly," she said. "I haven't been kidnapped. I'm right here. Really, Spencer. Haven't you stopped drinking yet?"

Dad Cole snatched the phone from Spencer's hand and stood staring at it, a menacing stillness about him. "My Love," Kate heard him mutter. She saw the blood recede from his face and thought he might fall over, but he recovered in time. He turned to Spencer, and waving his phone at him he shouted: "Who the hell is this texting you?"

Spencer sat down heavily and dropped his head to the table. He wrapped his arms around it as though trying to protect himself from the world. "Oh, God. What have I done?" he muttered into his serviette. "What have I done?"

"I don't know what you've done," Dad Cole yelled. "Who is this? And is it true?"

"Of course it's not true," Bridget snorted. "I'm here. Look at me. I'm here."

"Oh, Bridget!" Stella snapped. "Don't keep on. We know you're here. None of us could possibly miss that fact, could we? Of course you haven't been kidnapped. But if you haven't been kidnapped and this isn't a scam, then who has? Now, let me think. Oh, yes, your mother just left here in *your* car heading for *your* flat. Ooh, I wonder if maybe she's been mistaken for you. Can we please think of someone other than you just for a change?"

143

Bridget wasn't having it. "Don't be ridiculous! How could she possibly be mistaken for me? She's twice my age for a start."

Spencer's face hardened like quick-set concrete. He eyed Bridget as though she'd turned into a slug. "What did I ever see in you?" he said.

"Forget all that," Dad Cole snarled. "Who are these people? What are we dealing with here? Is this a scam? Some one's stupid idea of a joke? I want my wife back. If she's actually gone anywhere, that is. If she has, we must ring the police."

"No!" Spencer leapt from his seat and grabbed his phone back from Dad Cole. "We can't do that. They would kill her. This is my fault. But I know if we involve the police we'll never see Mum Cole again."

Most people in the room, including Kate, turned to look at Pete. Could he still be counted as police, being suspended as he was, she wondered? He'd know what to do in this situation, though, surely.

But he looked stymied and Kate had a sudden rush of sympathy for him. Maybe he was a corrupt policeman; maybe he wasn't. But whether he was or not, he was a suspended one with his entire career hanging in the balance. It seemed to her that most here tonight had thought the worst of him, including her, and yet when there was a sticky situation to be sorted – possibly a very, very sticky situation for Mum Cole – they all turned to him.

"No," Dad Benning said. He stepped forward and placed his hand on his son's shoulder. "I cannot have my son risk everything. You are asking too much. He's on suspension pending an enquiry. What exactly are you asking him to do that none of you could do instead?"

"It's all right, Dad," Pete muttered. "We need to get Mum Cole back."

"No, it's not all right. You're in enough trouble as it is."

"But, what about my wife?" Dad Cole demanded.

"You should have thought of your wife instead of neglecting her," Dad Benning said. "If not for that we wouldn't be in this situation in the first place. I'm quite prepared to help if I can, but I won't allow my son to sacrifice himself. I'm sorry about Mum Cole, but it's you who needs to rescue her. We will, of course, help, but the impetus must come from someone else."

Pete opened his mouth, but Dad Benning merely pressed even more firmly on his shoulder, and his son subsided.

Kate glanced in her mother's direction and found that she was staring at her husband, an expression on her face that looked strangely contented as though, at least this once, she could sit back and let him take control. It would seem everyone was finding out stuff about their nearest and dearest tonight that was coming as a surprise to them.

That was okay as long as it was nice stuff. Most of it, so far, hadn't been.

"So, who are these people, Spencer?" Dad Cole asked. "What have you got my wife into?"

"These people have been blackmailing me," Spencer said, his head sinking towards his hands again. He was brought up short by Dad Cole shaking him roughly. "Pull yourself together," he said. "This isn't about you. You've got an innocent woman in trouble. You've got to get her out of it."

Spencer said, "I needed money."

Kate, remembering Tom's hurt that his life-long friend and partner had swindled him, snorted, but said nothing.

Spencer heard it. "I'm sorry, Kate. I am so sorry that I stole from Tom. My best pal. I can't tell you how bad that makes me feel..."

He did look wretched, but Kate couldn't find it in herself to say anything that might make him feel better.

Dad Cole wasn't too impressed either. "Just at the moment that's not nearly as bad as my wife being terrified by some lowlife because of you," he said. "So quit with the self-indulgence and tell me what I need to know to get her back. Or I will have to go to the police."

Spencer looked up in shock. "It's not a good idea to go to the police. These people are only asking for money. You bring the police in and you'll never get her back."

"I'm no longer convinced," Dad Cole said. "You've proved yourself to be a lowlife yourself. How do I know I'm doing the right thing *not* getting onto the police straightaway? How do I know you're not just saying that to protect yourself from too-close scrutiny by the police?"

Spencer held his hands out in supplication to Pete, behind whom Errol and Clark both now stood. "Back me up, guys. You know what we're dealing with. Convince Dad Cole that calling the police is not the way to go."

Kate wondered what was going on. Were they all in on whatever it was? The three Hamilton boys plus her brother? They'd never been firm friends, any of them. The three Hamilton brothers had always half-heartedly hung together when needed, but they'd never appeared really close. And none of them had been bosom buddies with Pete. He'd always been a loner.

The only real friends in The Three Families had always been her and Bridget, which seemed stranger by the minute, and Tom and Spencer, which also seemed to be dissolving in front of her eyes.

Or had the others all been closer than she'd ever realised, and in her self-absorption with bits of fuchsia leaf and twig, she'd missed it.

"It's true, Dad Cole," Errol agreed. "These are nasty characters, if we're talking about who I think we're talking about, and bringing in the police won't help and is more likely to make things worse. Especially if it's just money they want out of Spencer. They've found him to be an easy target in the past and expect to cash in on him again. To get Mum Cole back, we'll just have to let them. It's the easiest and safest way out."

146

"You mean – you knew about Spencer getting in trouble before this and said nothing?" Dad Hamilton demanded, advancing on Errol.

"Forget it!" Dad Cole warned Dad Hamilton. "You can deal with your sons later. The important thing now is my wife. Spencer, how much do they want?"

"Two hundred thousand pounds," Spencer said, adding a whispered, "Sorry" that everyone ignored.

"Well!" Bridget said. "I hope they'd have wanted more than that if it had been me!" Everyone ignored her as well. Kate wondered if she was drunk.

But – crikey – that was a lot of money! Two hundred thousand... Silence fell on the room until a wailing cry from the corner announced Mum Hamilton descending into hysteria.

"Pull yourself together," Stella Benning said. "Your crocodile tears for Mum Cole aren't going to help."

But Dad Hamilton rushed to his wife's side, a position so recently vacated by Dad Cole.

Although realising the irony of Mum Hamilton's upset, Kate was conscious of some relief on hearing the sobs and little screams. Mum Hamilton's seemed to be the only really natural response to the fact that one of their number had been kidnapped. They were all standing around discussing it as though it was on a par with a flower trough being nicked from outside the house.

How was it that most of the people present were being so completely rational about it? Maybe they all felt so unreal they couldn't react normally, apart from Mum Hamilton. Or maybe they were all Zorros in disguise and merely took things in their stride and thundered off to the rescue. There's no room for hysterics when you're a hero.

Talking of which, it would be entirely acceptable if he were to put in an appearance now... She looked around hopefully but no masked, swashbuckling daredevil leapt into the room, Mum Cole safely slung across his broad shoulders. She sighed.

147

"Where do we take it?" Dad Cole was all business now there was something tangible he could do.

"You can get two hundred thousand so easily? Just like that?" Bridget wanted to know. Everyone ignored her.

"But if we give in to their demands this time," Marilyn said. "What's to stop them doing it again? What's to stop them kidnapping someone else and demanding more?"

"Let's get Mum Cole back first and worry about that afterwards, shall we?" Stella said, glancing worriedly at Dad Cole. He looked on the verge of detonation.

"How do we carry this out?" he demanded.

"There's an address in the Badlands. We take the money there and exchange it for Mum Cole," Spencer said.

Kate thought that sounded suspiciously simple, but maybe her ideas were clouded by reading too many crime novels.

"Who has to take it?"

"It has to be me, I'm afraid." Spencer shrugged and put on an exaggeratedly sorry face.

This was met with a silence so alive with meaning it shrieked energetic suspicion. No one was about to entrust Spencer Hamilton with two hundred thousand pounds after his admission of embezzlement during the caramel mousse ganache stage of the meal!

And to think that for all the years before this The Three Families had trusted each other without question. Well, as far as Kate was aware anyway... Maybe she really had been so wrapped up in her greenhouses and cuttings and pots of compost that The Three Families had all become crime lords over this time in competition with each other, and she'd missed it.

"The important thing is to get Mum Cole back," Spencer said as if they didn't know this.

No one was willing to state their distrust outright it would seem. "But how do we know for sure they *will* just hand her back?" Stella said. "Surely they're going to be afraid that we'll go to the police then. You seem to know who

148

they are, Spencer. What's to stop any of us going to the police about them afterwards?"

"We can't worry about these things now," Errol said. "First we have to get Mum Cole back. She must be terrified." He glanced a look of apology at Dad Cole as he said it, but of course she must be terrified. How could she not be?

Unless she was a crime lord herself and had set the whole thing up to get her hands on her husband's dosh. Kate just managed to stop herself snorting with laughter. But, really, nothing would surprise now, not after today's revelations. She wondered if it should be crime *lady* in that case...

"We're wasting time," Clark said. "Come on, Dad Cole. Let's get the dosh. Let's get this thing rolling."

It was interesting to see Clark being business-like and taking charge as though born to leadership. He'd always been a non-conformist, leaning away from close-knit associations, and yet here he was when he was needed, spearheading the rescue-Mum-Cole operation.

The Three Families headed for the front door and spilled out onto the garden path. The Hamiltons had come to the New Year's Day dinner in their SUV. Dad and Tom Cole, Clark, Spencer, and Errol Hamilton all headed for it.

Kate was glad to see that Mum and Dad Hamilton weren't coming along. Kate couldn't imagine either of them being very useful in a risky manoeuvre. They were both too laid back and unaware of how evil people could be. They were also ratarsed. Stella wasn't coming, of course, nor Bridget who had already gone back into the house.

Kate saw her dad physically hold back his son, shaking his head and talking urgently. Pete, with a darkly angry face slumped against the garden wall.

"I'm not happy about you going either," her dad said, turning to her.

"I'm the only one who hasn't drunk anything," Kate said. "There's no point getting stopped by the police on our way to the rescue. I'll drive." She expected no argument. It made sense. She hadn't wanted to be drunk in charge of a newly-acquired dog so for the first time in the history of The Three Families dinner, since she'd been an adult, she'd not had any alcohol.

Tom, staring at her dad as if trying to give him a message in his look, gripped her arm and said, "I'll make sure no harm comes to her."

All Kate wanted to do was throw his hand off her arm. Fancy talking about her like that as if she were a pathetic nitwit, or a possession! But she gritted her teeth and merely got into the driver's seat. Jeff-Dog jumped in to the passenger seat, tail waving delightedly as if they were off on an adventure. They just needed lashings of ginger beer, some corned beef and lettuce sandwiches in a hamper, and they'd have all the necessary gear. Kate made him get in the back where Clark held onto him, but not before he'd jumped onto Spencer and greeted him like a long lost friend.

"For God's sake! Why are you bringing that smelly mutt!" Spencer yelled.

Clark laughed. "Every adventure needs a dog," he said. "Anyway, he loves you. Why don't you love him?"

Why was Clark taunting Spencer? With difficulty because she didn't want to show her interest, Kate kept her eyes front and started the engine.

"Shut up you two. Now is not the time for bickering." Silence filled the vehicle. No one was going to argue with Dad Cole.

Reaching the Cole house everyone waited in the SUV while Dad Cole went in to get the money.

"Does this mean Dad Cole keeps that much cash in his house?" Spencer asked. "Surely not."

"He's just been paid for the Alsace job," Tom said.

"But he wouldn't go round telling people about it, would he?"

"No. It's very odd and I can't help feeling the kidnapper must have known about the money. He must have."

Spencer avoided his gaze. "How is it safe keeping that kind of money in his home?"

"It should be safe if it's only The Three Families who know about it. Although that's no longer a foregone conclusion, is it?" Tom said, bitterness tingeing his voice.

Spencer dropped his head. Kate looked away. It was sad to see a lifelong friendship in tatters like this.

Behind her, Errol asked: "But it's *not* safe for him to have that much money lying around."

It was a good point, but surely no one else's business but Dad Cole's, Kate thought. Having just been paid – in cash it would seem – he'd have been unable to deposit it yet. It was a time of bank holidays and irregular opening hours. Although why he'd have been paid in cash was a puzzle… Kate couldn't believe there was anything dodgy about Dad Cole's business…

She turned around to ask Tom and was struck by the fact she couldn't see anything except pale blobs for faces and the white of Jeff-Dog's neck ruff. She hadn't noticed before, but everyone was wearing black: black trousers, black shoes, black tops of one sort or another; their individual outfits varying in sartorial elegance, but all black.

That surely couldn't be coincidence. Could it?

She'd been getting a suspicion that someone knew something about this evening that she didn't, but now she knew for certain that everyone knew something she didn't!

What the hell was going on?

She opened her mouth to demand answers but Tom's hand on her shoulder increased its pressure and the look he gave her, his face very close to hers, kept Kate quiet. Nope. She had *no* idea what was going on!

Finally, a shadow darker than the rest moved towards them and Dad Cole, who had apparently changed into an entirely black outfit, too, climbed into the vehicle, his weight making it dip slightly on the passenger side.

Without saying anything, Kate turned the key in the ignition and waited for directions from someone. The four in the back were mumbling about something she couldn't catch, but as she watched them in the rear-view mirror Spencer looked up. "Head for where you got Rover," he said.

151

A chill swept over Kate and she couldn't look away from Spencer's eyes in the mirror. How did he know anything about her and a dog called Rover, let alone where she'd got him from?

Chapter Nineteen

Kate shook her gaze free from Spencer's eyes in the rear view mirror, released the handbrake and pulled out into the road hoping, without much conviction, that he wouldn't have noticed her realisation of his slip.

Spencer should know nothing about Rover or about her escapades of the night before. As far as he was concerned, she'd turned up tonight with a dog that *wasn't* Rover, a dog called Jeff that she *hadn't* got from the Badlands at all.

Could it be that Spencer had recognised Jeff-Dog as Rover because he didn't have his balaclava on? Even if he had, how did he know Rover in the first place? Come to think of it, Jeff-Dog had certainly behaved as if he knew Spencer…

No one else had witnessed their silent exchange judging by the uninterrupted mumbling going on amongst the others. Kate kept driving, her mind a jumble of shock and new ideas about Spencer, that couldn't possibly be true. Could they?

He was Zorro!!! He had to be Zorro.

And if it was Spencer, that explained a few things. She'd never thought him fanciable in all her growing-up years, but now she looked at him differently, she could see that he could be. How could anyone who had rescued a dog for her *not* be fanciable? Heat replaced the chill encasing her body as she looked at him for too long in her mirror. He frowned horribly at her and she allowed herself a little smile back at him and lifted her hand in what she thought was a subtle thumbs-up gesture. She would keep his confidence. He needn't worry. She wasn't about to betray her hero!

153

She remembered the way to Jeff-Dog's House of Hell very well. When she could see the police tape cordoning off the area around it, she stopped in the road, Spencer leapt out and unfastened the flimsy barrier so she could drive through; he reattached the tape and jumped back into the vehicle. Reaching their destination Kate switched off the engine.

No one moved or spoke until Spencer held out his hand to Dad Cole who gave him the bag which presumably contained the two hundred thousand pounds. What if it didn't?

Which is when Kate remembered again that Spencer was supposed to have embezzled Tom out of a lot of money. How could her hero be an embezzler? The simple answer was that he wasn't. Tom himself had said that the way Spencer had done it made it apparent that something else was going on, and that he wanted to be caught.

She would have faith in her hero and not let doubts ruin this wonderful feeling she had of having finally found the right one for her. She sent him a little smile and he pretended not to see it. She had known he would. Kate's heart leapt with the excitement of it all. They had a definite bond and it was thrilling to know she had such a close connection with him.

But, really, what did she know of love and its finer mysteries? She'd always thought she was in love with Tom and look what happened to that idea. It had been suffocated in an over-possessive clinginess she simply couldn't cope with.

And, anyway, how did one really know if one were in love or not? You might want to throw yourself in front of a runaway truck to protect the one you loved but you might do it just because you couldn't think what else to do and yet something had to be done. Or maybe you only tripped in its way and got squished for no good reason. And anyway, would your body be enough to stop a runaway truck from squishing someone else's too? No. Why would it? It would just plough through you and then plough through them as well so where was the point in the first place? That settled that then. She wasn't going to throw herself in front of a speeding truck for anyone!

Spencer hesitated, his hand on the car door. "It says in the text that it has to be me that takes the money to the house," Spencer said, carefully not looking at Kate. "I'd better get to it, then. Is there a plan? I mean, what if they take the money, but don't hand over Mum Cole? Or, what if they shoot me, grab the money and don't hand over Mum Cole? Have we a plan?" He tailed off and waited for someone to come to his rescue, to reassure him they would be there for him. But apparently no one wanted to.

Kate was aghast. What was wrong with these people? They'd all known each other their entire lives. They were all on the same side weren't they! Surely they had a plan! Fate obviously had set up this opening for her to help out her man. She stared at Spencer, willing him to pick up her unspoken message. "I'll come with you. And Jeff-Dog. Then there'll be three of us and it won't be so easy for them to pull a fast one." *And we will face whatever happens together, a united front, a couple and their dog against the world.*

But her hero, predictably enough, didn't want her to be in any danger and he dismissed her suggestion out of hand with just enough contempt to cover up their secret understanding. "Well, thanks for that, Kate, but I hardly think you or your only-too-eager-to-please dog is going to scare them into keeping their arrangement."

Dad Cole was shaking his head but said nothing.

"No, Kate," Tom said. "You're not going."

Before Kate could argue Clark chimed in as well! "You're not going, Kate," he said. "No one can go with Spencer. The kidnappers have asked for him. Having someone else show up, too, will spook them. Our best chance is to do what they've asked. If it goes tits up after that then we'll have to think again."

"By which time I might have been killed," Spencer said. "Thanks."

"Possibly," Errol said. "But you mess with people like this and you pay the price." Spencer gave him such a filthy look Kate was surprised Errol didn't melt into a pool of grease on the seat.

She was still outraged at Tom's and Clark's high-handed disposal of her intentions, though. "It's not for you lot to say what I can and what I can't do!" she announced, but a beeping announced a text arriving and everyone fell silent.

They watched Spencer as he slowly retrieved his mobile phone and perused the screen, the light from it glowing in the dark of the SUV. When he looked up his features were in deep shadow like when they'd shone a torch under their chins as children trying to scare each other. Kate was spooked all right, this time for real. He looked demonic, but then, so would Zorro in some lights.

"They know we're here," he said in a low voice as though whoever 'they' were could hear him. "They're watching us."

Everyone looked around as though 'they' were going to let themselves be spotted.

"They want Kate and the dog to come with me when I take the money."

"No!" Tom and Clark said in unison.

"Why?" Dad Cole queried without, it would seem, any hope of getting an answer.

"We're here because we've decided to do what they want to get Mum Cole back," Kate said, trying not to be smug over Tom and Clark being thwarted so easily. "So we must do what they want."

"You're very kind, Kate," Dad Cole said. "But only go if you feel you want to. It seems odd to me that they've specified you and your dog…"

"Of course I want to," she said, briefly clasping his arm in reassurance.

"But why would they want you and the dog to go with Spencer?" Tom asked.

"Why have they only asked for two hundred thousand when they could have asked for four or five, or more?" Errol said. "None of any of this makes sense. So we might as well just go along with it."

156

"Let's go then," Kate said opening her door. "No point in putting it off." And, anyway, Zorro was bound to have some daring plan to rescue Mum Cole and the money and resolve the entire situation when they got to their destination. She wanted to see him in action. And she wanted a chance to be on her own with him even if only for the short trip up to the house.

She was conscious of the others also leaving the car. They melted into the deep shadows of the bushes and surrounding hedges.

They set off, Kate carefully keeping Jeff-Dog between them so that she wouldn't forget discretion and grab Zorro's hand. And, of course, Kate realised, that was why Jeff-Dog had behaved as though he knew Spencer. He *did* know him! He'd been rescued by him. Things were fitting nicely into place now she finally had all the facts.

Being the gentleman he was, Spencer automatically stood back to let Kate walk up the garden path ahead of him. She was conscious of him close behind her wanting to overtake when he realised she would be first at the door, but she deliberately walked in erratic fashion to stop him. She could do her bit to protect her hero too. It wasn't all down to him, although she was a bit worried about Jeff-Dog and wished she'd left him in the car.

She needn't have worried. As they approached the house, the door opened, Jeff-Dog let out an excited yip and leapt on to the person holding it back so welcomingly. It was Weasel-Face! Jeff-Dog was really pleased to see him. That dog wasn't picky enough for his own good! He was convinced the world was only populated by wonderful people. Kate wished she could have that optimism in her fellow humans. At least Zorro had brought a little of that back into her life, though. She smiled at the thought and Weasel-Face smiled back at her. It was a scary sight.

"You've brought the dog back. Quite right, too. You can't have your measly couple of hundred quid back, though. He's worth way more than that!" Smugness made his weaselly features even more pronounced.

157

Kate stopped smiling. Weasel-Face was a baddie! What was she thinking going off into her dream world of heroes and swashbuckling when there were people like Weasel-Face about the place?

"Where is Mum Cole?" she demanded.

"Who?" he said.

"Your hostage! You know, the reason why we've brought the dosh."

He scratched his head like a mime of cartoon puzzlement. "What?"

"Well, don't just stand there – go and get her!"

"You're demented," he declared. "If you mean Bridget, you can't have her, but I'll have the dog back." And he snatched Jeff-Dog's lead from her hand and disappeared into the house.

It took Kate a moment to realise what had happened. "Oy!" she shrieked and ran after him. Jeff-Dog was bounding along with Weasel-Face as though it was a game! And where was Zorro when she needed him? She glanced behind her but there was no sign of Spencer. She stopped. He must have been taken by the baddies because Weasel-Face hadn't taken the money so Spencer must still have it! She looked after Jeff-Dog and thought about Zorro, and she ran after her hound. Zorro could look after himself!

Kate felt some shame at her desertion but maybe Zorro wasn't her hero after all. He hadn't behaved very heroically just now had he? He'd let her go first into this house of wickedness instead of shielding her from it. Yes, she'd just fallen out of love with him, which was quite a relief. She never had fancied Spencer. And now she knew she'd been right all along.

What had she been thinking? It was time to get her priorities straight, and her priorities consisted of her dog and her fuchsia cuttings, and to hell with what anyone else thought of it!

Chapter Twenty

She raced down the corridor after Weasel-Face and the prancing shadow that accompanied him. She just had time to think what a long corridor it was for such a small house, and how peculiar, and had she been whisked into a parallel dimension by some otherworldly force, when something came down over her head blocking out all sight; iron bands went around her body pinning her arms to her torso. She was trussed!

She tried to kick her assailant by swinging her heel back and was gratified to hear a curse as she connected with what she hoped was his shin. She squirmed and writhed as far as she was able and swung her heel back again, but finally it got through to her that her captor was whispering over and over: "Stop. Stop. Stop. It's me."

Zorro? Kate stopped struggling. "What are you doing?" she demanded. "Weasel-Face is getting away with Jeff-Dog!"

"He'll be fine."

"How do you know?"

There was no answer forthcoming, it would seem. Kate pulled at the fabric that enveloped her head. It felt satiny and insubstantial but she couldn't shift it. "Get it off! Get it off!" she yelled, panic setting in as the thing clung to her face and refused to budge.

"No, leave it," he said. "You must keep it on. If you see what you're not supposed to see, you'll in much worse danger than you are already."

"What are you on about?" she hissed, still yanking at the material with no discernible effect whatsoever. "I just want my dog back."

159

Zorro – if it was him – was hanging on to the hood while she was trying to dislodge it and his voice came out in a highly unromantic, wavery wail: "You'll get him back! He'll be fine. They just want the information he has, that's all."

"Information?" pictures flashed through her mind of her poor dog manacled to a chair, subjected to bright lights and harsh interrogation and him just giving his rank and number and refusing to give the location of the bones he'd buried. After all, what other information could he possibly have?

There was no way that dog would break and divulge everything he knew, and then things would get worse. "Don't be ridiculous!" she snapped, not sure whether she was talking to herself or to him. "What information could Jeff-Dog possibly have that a drug lord would be interested in?" She had to assume it was a drug lord given where they were...

Zorro appeared to have no answer to this so Kate took advantage of his nonplussed silence to kick out again. The whole masked hero thing was so yesterday and she was so over it! She'd grown out of it very fast which gave her an instant's flash of pride at her grownupedness. But only an instant. How daft the whole thing had been, especially given the current situation of her dog being abducted and Zorro not only not helping to save him but stopping her from going in pursuit.

Filled with renewed determination she stamped on his foot only to find it was no longer there. In fact, he was no longer there at all – no part of him – and her arms were free again, too. She wrestled the hood off her head and was immediately blinded by the light in the corridor. She could however make out a black shadow bounding towards her yelping with glee. Oh, thank heaven! She fell to her knees and Jeff-Dog ran into her arms and snuffled excitedly through her hair as if searching for hidden treats.

She'd had no idea when she set out to foster dogs how fast one such hound could take her over and become so much a part of her she would rather cut off her own leg with a rusty potato peeler than lose him. She hugged him harder and he responded by trying to lick her ear off her head. Kate brought her hands up to stop this impromptu and not entirely appreciated ear-wash and suddenly realised Jeff-Dog had his balaclava back on.

What the hell!?!

He'd been abducted; she'd been hooded and restrained for what – ten minutes? Fifteen? – all so someone could restore her dog's balaclava to him. It made no sense at all! Maybe all this really wasn't happening. Maybe she was in actual fact ill and hallucinating or maybe she was still at home in bed and hadn't left it at all in the last thirty-six hours.

She looked around, curious to see what was so dangerous for her to see, but there was nothing but a corridor with several doors leading off. It made her feel even more unreal because she knew there was no way Rover's House of Hell was anywhere near big enough for such a corridor. Maybe it was a warp in the fabric of time and space but her suspicion was that someone had connected all the houses in this terrace by tunnelling through the adjoining walls, which, she had to admit, was a good idea if this was indeed the headquarters for a drug empire.

Although tempted to explore she thought it wiser to get Jeff-Dog to a place of safety first where he was less likely to be abducted for what he knew. She snorted. How ridiculous! What could Jeff-Dog possibly know that anyone other than a rival hound would want to know?

Also, there was Mum Cole to worry about...

Chapter Twenty-one

Having lost all sense of direction whilst imprisoned by Zorro, Kate simply opened the first door she came to, and found herself facing a cosily domestic scene in a large kitchen that looked as though it had been tacked onto the house as an afterthought.

Weasel-Face was fussing around with a teapot trying to get a lacy lime green tea cosy over its spout. Mum Cole sat at the table. She looked comfortable, not at all like someone there under duress, or someone Kate needed to worry about. Jeff-Dog, with a yelp of delight, shot across the room and greeted Mum Cole with exuberant joy. She seemed just as enchanted to see him as he was to see her.

"Hello Kate," Mum Cole said. "Now you're here, everything will work out. Don't look so worried." She patted the chair next to hers and went back to scratching Jeff-Dog's neck under his balaclava. He sat, eyes blissfully closed, leaning into her leg. It was a scene of domestic harmony, not at all what one might expect when it included a stolen dog in disguise, a woman kidnapped in place of her daughter, and a drug dealer.

Not convinced that she wasn't in fact at home, in bed, delirious with fever, Kate sat down at the table. Mum Cole smiled at her, but said nothing.

Kate was at a loss. She'd like to know what the hell was going on, but it didn't look like anyone was going to tell her any time soon. Weasel-Face joined them at the table bearing a tray with cups and saucers and all the usual paraphernalia for a nice cup of tea. There was even a plate of macaroons. Lovely.

"Uh… So, what's what then?" she enquired, trying to keep her tone level so as not to set off any unruly emotions. After all, they were only sitting in a drug hell-hole with a kidnapper and his victim. Anything could happen.

"We're waiting for the money to show up and then Bridget can go," Weasel-Face informed her, busily pouring milk into cups.

"Bridget?" Kate queried.

"Yes, love," Mum Cole gave her a warning look and Kate was struck by the thought that she really was supposed to be Bridget. Oh.

"Uh, are you all right? Have they treated you okay?" Kate tried to call Mum Cole Bridget but the name stuck in her throat.

"Fine," Mum Cole said. "It's only a business arrangement."

Was this truly the woman who only moments ago had been lying on a bed sodden with her tears? Kate was beginning to see her in a whole new light after she'd had a go at her daughter, faced down her two-timing husband, and now sat so calmly sipping tea in the middle of this den of vice.

"Yeah. Course," Weasel-Face said. "If we'd known Spencer's tastes ran to the more mature woman we'd have been even more prepared – we could have provided a two-handled cup for your tea, Bridget, even a special pressure-relief cushion. If we'd had more notice even one of those chairs that throws you out of them when you want to get up, and can't." He laughed uproariously, in weasel-fashion, slopping his tea over the table, wiping mirthful tears from his eyes and ignoring his guests' stony silence.

Spencer appeared in the doorway and abruptly Weasel-Face sobered up, but not soon enough. "I heard you," Spencer said. "I'd watch it if I were you. The age difference between me and Bridget can't be much bigger than the age difference between you and your bit of stuff."

"My bit of stuff!" Weasel-Face gasped. "Say that in front of her. I dare you!"

163

Watching with vast interest Kate was certain Spencer paled. She wondered who Weasel's bit of stuff was. She wondered who on earth would *be* Weasel's bit of stuff. She looked at him with narrowed eye, but no, she couldn't see it. She couldn't see what anyone would fancy in that quarter.

"Right. Let's get out of here," Spencer said, helping Mum Cole with her chair, not that she needed it, but he'd been well brought up. Kate caught a smug grin on Weasel's face. Before it made her cross she stopped looking at it and bent over to retrieve Jeff-Dog's lead, which was still attached to his collar. She headed for the door after Spencer and Mum Cole, but as Kate reached it a shadow materialized and blocked her way.

"Just a minute," the shadow said. It was Errol Hamilton. He was wearing all black and something that looked suspiciously like a balaclava hung from his belt. This was getting very confusing!

"I'm taking the dog," Errol continued, and snatched the lead from Kate's hand. She stood a moment shocked into immobility. But then, she snatched the lead back. "No, you're not!" she snapped. "You didn't even want to talk to him at the dinner. He's my dog now. And he's staying my dog! You don't even like dogs."

"I like this one," he said, and snatched the lead back again from Kate's hand.

"What the hell?" Kate said. "Why the sudden interest?" Errol was behaving in a very odd way. He was never usually this assertive, at least amongst The Three Families. She leant forward and grabbed the lead back again whereupon Jeff-Dog jumped up barking delightedly at this new lark. Errol stepped closer to Kate. She stepped back and fell over Weasel's foot.

"He wants the dog, he has the dog," Weasel announced grandly standing over Kate as she lay stunned on the floor, said dog slumped on her chest trying to give her a good facial scrub with his slobbery tongue. She fought him off and heaved herself to her feet to find that Dad Hamilton had appeared now, too. Where had he come from? And how come he wasn't weaving about the place and slobbering given how ratarsed he'd been last time she'd seen him back at the ranch?

"No, he doesn't have to have the dog," Dad Hamilton announced. "He doesn't want it either."

"Yes, I do," Errol said, a trifle sulkily Kate thought.

Weasel and Dad Hamilton were eyeballing each other as if they were stags about to lock horns and fight to the death. What the hell? But, even though she'd like to know what that was about she was conscious that if they decided to work together with Errol to take her down and commandeer Jeff-Dog they could, so she ran like a greyhound for the door, the lead still firmly clenched in her hand. Her hairy co-conspirator barked loudly sensing yet another caper in his near future; enthralled he hurled himself after her.

She still heard Dad Hamilton's yelling something about "...an old dog..." followed by Weasel-Face yelling something back, followed by a thwacking noise. What the hell?

But her focus switched instantly to the black-clad and suitably masked figure which stepped into the breach behind her, thus preventing any pursuit of her. She risked a quick glance back, realized Zorro had come to her rescue again and sprinted out of the house dragging Jeff-Dog with her. He had wanted to greet Zorro, but Kate had no time for such niceties.

At least now she could be certain her Zorro wasn't Dad Hamilton. Or Weasel-Face. Or Errol. But she couldn't be certain of anything else...

She also wondered about the advisability of leaving Dad Hamilton alone with Weasel-Face, but they had seemed to know each other, and if needed, she was sure that Zorro would rescue him now he was here. In the meantime, she'd reached the outside of the house in time to witness several black-clad and masked figures milling around. How did they know who was who? She hadn't a clue. Uncertainty gripped her again. Maybe the Zorro that had just rescued her wasn't her Zorro... Maybe it was another Zorro? How many Zorros were there fer cryin' out loud?

Pete was there as well. And he was definitely not supposed to be. What was he doing? What was going on? Did she really care? Oh, how she longed for her greenhouse...

The next minute Dad Cole was shaking her. "Kate! Where's Mum Cole?"

"She's with Spencer. They left the house before I did."

"Where's Spencer?"

"Uh..." Kate looked around wildly trying to spot either Spencer or Mum Cole but couldn't see them. "They must have come out first."

"Nope. No one came out until you did," he said and ran into the house.

As if that had been a pre-arranged signal, everyone piled into the house. Kate followed. She thought she might as well, if only to try and find out what was going on! Even if her Zorro wasn't amongst the assembled black-clad company, she surely would be safe in there in the middle of this number of Three Families people. She traipsed through to the kitchen, her trusty dog by her side, and sat on the only empty chair.

Mum Cole was once more at the table, Dad Cole by her side. He was holding her hand as if he'd never let it go. There was no sign of Spencer. Idly, Kate wondered where the money was.

Weasel-Face stood near the sink holding a wet cloth to his bleeding nose and flicking sideways glances at Mum and Dad Cole's joined hands. It didn't take long for Kate to realise it was because he thought Mum Cole was actually Bridget, and Bridget was Spencer's girlfriend. So what was she doing holding hands with Dad Cole in Weasel-Face's kitchen? And he'd already got in enough trouble, it seemed, with Dad Hamilton, who was also at the sink bathing grazed knuckles under the running tap.

Now Weasel-Face was surrounded by most of the members of The Three Families, too, and yet he remained more concerned about 'Bridget' holding hands with the wrong man, than he did about his own safety. Kate found this very puzzling.

Everyone else arranged themselves around the walls and it was as if they all waited for something to happen…

Dad Hamilton broke the silence. "So, why aren't you out there, Tom, with Clark and Pete, chasing Spencer down and getting the money back? It's quite a bit of money, after all!"

"What money?" Weasel-Face asked. "The money never turned up! Is someone holding out on me?"

"What are you doing here anyway, Dad Hamilton?" Tom asked. Kate noticed he avoided Weasel-Face's question. "You were – apparently – absolutely plastered before we left the Bennings' house and it was decided you'd be better off staying there. And yet, somehow, here you are. How is that?"

"I was worried about Mum Cole," Dad Hamilton said. "Your mother. Remember her? She was kidnapped. Remember that?" He raised his skinned knuckles as if to say he'd taken on the baddie in Mum Cole's defence even if no one else could be bothered.

But Kate knew it was nothing to do with Mum Cole that he'd attacked Weasel-Face. It was something to do with an old dog. She was still puzzling over it.

"Mum Cole – who's that?" Weasel-Face demanded, bewilderment stark on his face.

"So, you sobered up. Just like that," Tom said, still ignoring Weasel-Face. "And then you got here – how, exactly?"

"What do you mean the money never turned up?'" Kate asked Weasel-Face.

"Yes, what do you mean?" Dad Hamilton asked turning to Weasel-Face. "That is why you kidnapped Mum Cole, after all. You can't pretend innocence now."

"Mum Cole. Who the hell *is* that?" Weasel-Face yelled as if at the end of his endurance with this unasked-for company. He waved his hand in Mum Cole's direction. "We kidnapped Spencer's girlfriend so that we could get the dog back!"

"The dog?" Kate squeaked, clutching hard to Jeff-Dog's collar. "What dog?" She looked around wildly as if another dog would appear and no one would notice the one already there.

"Spencer's girlfriend?" Dad Hamilton repeated staring at Mum Cole, undisguised horror etched on his face.

Mum Cole laughed and shook her head. Dad Cole kissed her face and gave Dad Hamilton a what-an-idiot-you-are look.

"That dog!" Weasel-Face shouted, pointing at Jeff-Dog who woofed acknowledgement at being the centre of attention again. It was only right. "Rover. Of course. And now we've got him I reckon the rest of you lot can bugger off. Dunno what you're doing sitting around in my place anyway. Drinking my tea." He sounded most aggrieved.

"No, you're right," Kate said. "We wouldn't like to outstay our welcome." She stood up, her chair screeching on the floor, and made for the door only to find Weasel-Face had got there before her.

"Not you," he said. "At least, you can go, but Rover stays."

"Nope. Not gonna happen," she said stepping to the side only to be thwarted by him stepping to the side, too. She stared at him but he merely smirked back at her. Where the hell was Zorro when she needed him?

"Is that Rover, Kate?" Tom, suddenly at her shoulder, asked, nodding towards her canine companion.

"No, it's not!" she said. "It's Jeff-Dog. Rover has no brown on him."

"You have no claim," Tom said to Weasel-Face. "Let her go."

"The brown on that dog is just dye," Weasel-Face said. "It's an impostor. It is actually my dog, Rover."

"Are you calling my fiancée a liar?" Tom said, squaring up to him.

Kate had a moment of warm gratefulness to Tom – even though he'd called her 'his fiancée' in that awful possessive way he'd recently developed as if she were some sort of belonging like a lawnmower or a gas-powered barbecue.

But a commotion out in the hall saved Weasel-Face from answering, and the others appeared. Kate registered the fleeting look of anxiety that flashed across Tom's face when Clark and Pete bowled into the room. She also noted the equally momentary look of relief when Pete announced that Spencer had got away. What was that about?

"With the money?" Dad Hamilton wanted to know.

"With the money," Pete affirmed.

Yes, Tom definitely looked relieved. Almost pleased, in fact. How very odd. Kate was going to be interrogating him when the opportunity arose, that was for sure!

Chapter Twenty-two

Then Zorro turned up and Kate's heart stuttered, stopped, speeded up and then decided that it would in fact keep on beating. Especially when Zorro peeled his balaclava off to show Errol's face underneath.

Surely her Zorro wasn't Errol, after all? That would be too awful. But no, it was merely the trendy outfit of this year's New Year season, the whole black everything plus balaclava thing. Not only that, but Errol was carrying some poo bags. Used ones by the look of it. Why would he be doing that? If there was one thing she was certain of it was that her Zorro wouldn't be making a collection of used poo bags.

She didn't even know Errol had a dog.

"Didn't know you had a dog, son," Dad Hamilton said.

"Of course I haven't! Horrible hairy, dirty things! It's his," he said, gesturing at Jeff-Dog who grinned at him.

Kate thought it must be quite a compliment to a dog to have its poo all bagged up and treasured in this way.

"Why are you hanging on to all that poo, then, if you hate dogs so much?" Kate asked.

"Because it's got the chip in it," Errol said triumphantly.

The chip? "Wouldn't a chip have been digested by the time it got to the poo stage?" Kate said. Her head felt as though it was going to explode any minute. It was all too puzzling for comfort.

"Not that kind of chip, you daft apath! A silicon chip."

This didn't help her much. She was pleased to hear that Jeff-Dog was microchipped, but entirely failed to see how it came to pass through his digestive system. Surely that made it a bit inefficient. She didn't have the energy to question it.

Someone else did, though. A new voice cut through the mumblings in the room as Mum Hamilton appeared in the doorway. "The chip, Errol?" she said staring at him until he flushed and lowered his head. "You have it?"

Weasel-Face grabbed a chair and rushed over to her, setting it down carefully just inside the door. Mum Hamilton completely ignored him, didn't even thank him for his efforts, and moved it across the doorway as if to block it entirely. Then she sat on it in the silence that had fallen, pulled her voluminous handbag from her shoulder, opened it, rootled about in it, pulled out a gun, dropped her bag on the floor and smiled at the stunned crowd before her.

"Just so we're clear. This is a gun," she said, waving it about in a way that made Kate feel quite jumpy. Not that she'd know if it really was a gun, or a fake gun come to that. She wasn't prepared to mess with it anyway. "And I know how to use it," Mum Hamilton continued. "And I won't hesitate to use it if I see fit."

Kate backed away dragging Jeff-Dog with her. He was desperate to say hello to Mum Hamilton. But if she didn't know whether a gun was fake or not she was pretty certain he didn't so she made him come with her even though he didn't thank her for it.

One thing was for sure – next time she came down with a flu or cold or whatever this was she definitely was not going to leave her bed until she was completely clear of it. All this hallucinating had to be down to her not resting properly.

"So, Errol," Mum Hamilton said. "Do you have the chip?"

"I should do," he mumbled raising the bags of poo higher to indicate that it was in one of them.

"But you don't know? You haven't been through them?"

"Not yet. I was thinking a sieve might be a good thing to use. I don't have a sieve. I thought there might be one in here." He looked around the room as if a sieve would leap out of a cupboard and present itself for use in filtering dog poo.

"The dog that laid the golden crap!" Weasel-Face said, and laughed loudly. Until Mum Hamilton speared him with a look which made him suddenly stop and lower his head. Kate felt she should be surprised at how Mum Hamilton was dominating the proceedings but she wasn't. Not at all. And it wasn't just the gun. There was something about her she'd never seen before, and would never have suspected lurked beneath that soft, mild-mannered façade.

Mum Hamilton had always been unremarkable in every way except for her obsession with old movie stars, and yet here she was exhibiting a sinister inflexibility terrifying in its complete naturalness. She'd assumed it like shrugging on a well-worn cardigan.

"Am I really leaving my empire in your hands?" Mum Hamilton asked Errol, wonderment in her voice. "Tell me, have you been following that dog around catching its crap since Wisley got shot of it?"

"Um..." Errol shifted from foot to foot.

Mum Hamilton gave Weasel-Face a look that promised retribution later. "Not that he should have got shot of it, of course." She turned back to her hapless son: "You've been following this dog around all this time. I mean, are you sure you've got every single poop he's pooped?"

"Yep," Errol asserted proudly.

Mum Hamilton sighed. "I have a nasty feeling I'm going to regret asking this, but I have to ask this... Why? Errol. Why? Why have you done this thing?"

"I saw the note Wisley left for me," he said, staring at his mother as if hypnotised by her.

"I didn't leave a note for you, Errol!" Weasel-Face declared.

"No," Mum Hamilton said. "I left a note for *you*, Wisley! Whatever possessed you to leave it lying around? Why didn't you take it with you or destroy it?"

"I think it might have fallen on the floor," he mumbled defensively. "I was desperate to get the dog back, and I didn't think of the note again…"

Mum Hamilton gave his excuse her considered and subtle reply: "Dickhead!"

Weasel-Face cringed, dropped his gaze and shuffled his feet.

Kate flinched. She wasn't used to that kind of language from any of The Three Families parents. But then, she wasn't used to knowing people who sat around holding a gun, or being in a drug den or who had any familiarity with this kind of situation at all!

She noticed Dad Hamilton smirk, until he found his wife's glare directed at him, whereupon he backed up a couple of steps. The wall prevented him going any further.

Switching back to her son, Mum Hamilton said, "Even if you did find the note, Errol, what was there in it that possessed you to pick up the dog's poo?" She wrinkled her nose as if said dog's poo steamed directly under it.

"The note clearly said: 'The chip's in the dog'. Obviously that meant collecting up all its poo and anything else exiting from its body for at least twenty-four hours in order to make sure I found it. The chip, that is."

Mum Hamilton's expression was difficult to interpret. Kate fancied it was a struggle between disbelief and utter contempt. "You really thought the dog ate the chip?" she queried, apparently trying to work her way through her youngest son's thought processes.

"Of course," he said. "Like when you leave me a note that says: 'Your supper's in the dog' – it was obviously the same thing."

Kate almost felt sorry for Errol. He looked so bewildered.

"I should make you go through it, really, if there was any justice…" Mum Hamilton murmured.

173

"Would he know it if he saw it?" Weasel-Face asked.

"Nah," she said. "The only chip he knows anything about would have salt and vinegar on it and wouldn't survive the passage through a dog's gullet and out the other side. As it were."

Uncertainty flashed across Errol Hamilton's face.

"See," Mum Hamilton crowed. "He hadn't even thought of that. He never was the brightest bauble on the tree – to use a nicely seasonal metaphor."

"No, I hadn't," he agreed, face drooping. "Of course that wouldn't work. The chip wouldn't come out the other end untouched would it!" He smacked his forehead in exasperation with himself. "All your contact information, all the names, all the numbers, all the dirt you've got on them would end up in the dog's intestines, not in a pile of crap somewhere." Savagely, he drop-kicked a bag of poo. In its flight, it rustled past Kate's ear, hit the wall behind her with a horribly squelchy sound, and slid down to land on the floor. Jeff-Dog sniffed at it and backed away, lip curling up from his teeth.

"Exactly!" Mum Hamilton beamed at him as if he had gained status as her favourite pupil.

Whereupon he straightened up with his own broad grin threatening to split his face. "Exactly," he agreed. "Pity I'm not the brightest bauble on the tree, isn't it," he said. "Or I could have got you to confess you'd put all your contact information on that chip. The one you implanted into Rover's neck, that is. Oh. Oops!" Theatrically he put the back of his hand to his forehead. "That's what I seem to have done! Not only that but it's all recorded, too, and has been heard by everyone in The Three Families who are here and also the ones listening to speaker-phone elsewhere. Sorry, Mum. I'm such a fool."

Mum Hamilton stilled, paled, reddened, paled again, lifted the gun from her lap and shot her son in the leg. He fell to the floor clutching his maimed limb, gasping in little breaths.

"I never could abide a smart aleck," Mum Hamilton announced. "I'm off now. With my lover and my fortune. I won't see any of you again."

But Dad Hamilton wanted a word, too. While the rest of the company remained in mute, immobile shock, he announced: "And I'm going to let you go. Take note of that – I am letting you go. This is my final act as your husband and the father of your children because I believe it's better for you to be completely out of their lives than in prison here. But if I find out that you're back in the UK or in touch with any of them in any way then I will make sure you are captured and locked up forever."

Mum Hamilton looked a tad gobsmacked for a second. Probably as gobsmacked as the rest of them that her husband had finally grown a pair. But she wasn't quiet for long: "They're not your children!" she spat.

"You think I don't know that? Biologically they might not be. I've always known. But in every other way they are more mine than yours. Now piss off!" He stooped over Errol and pressed his hand to his son's injured leg.

Kate tried very hard not to catch anyone's eye but she just knew everyone would be looking at Dad Cole. Sure enough there was an exasperated snort, and Dad Cole said: "Don't be ridiculous. I'm not responsible for *all* of them. I *am* responsible for Clark. And proud of it." Kate peered up under her lashes to see how Mum Cole was taking this; she clutched her husband's hand and smiled approvingly at him.

"At least I always knew I wasn't," Clark said, holding the door open for his mother and Weasel-Face to leave. "I feel sorry for the rest of my charming siblings only finding out now, but it might even be good for them. Might even help broaden their characters a little. God knows – they could do with it." He laughed. No one joined him.

"Uh – too soon?" he enquired innocently, and winked at Kate.

But she was too puzzled by so many unanswered questions to appreciate levity just yet. "So, why is Mum Hamilton behaving like this?" She asked the room at large, unable to actually look at the woman in question. Respect for their elders had so thoroughly been drilled into her that she still couldn't see Mum Hamilton as anything other than a Three Families mother as yet.

"She runs a drug ring called the 'Counters'," Dad Hamilton offered tiredly. "It would seem she's been at it for years under cover of being a Stepford wife."

'Counters'? Why would they be called 'Counters'? The word made Kate think of tiddlywinks and shop counters. She wasn't sure either would be relevant in this context. She was distracted by Weasel-Face asking: "A Stepford wife? What the hell is a Stepford wife?"

"Oh, you know – a submissive and docile wife who makes her own chutney, sews her own lace doilies, whose children are always clean and who always has supper on the table for hubbie whatever time he gets home," Clark said.

Kate had to admire Weasel-Face's restraint as he stared at Clark and then at Mum Hamilton and then back at Clark. And said absolutely nothing. His face said it all. It would seem Mum Hamilton had never made chutney for the Counters' cheese sandwiches.

"And you must admit, my Victoria sponges were to die for," Mum Hamilton said fluttering her hands in an obscene parody of her previous persona. The assembled company received this reminder of the old and well-loved Mum Hamilton in stony silence: the current Mum Hamilton still had a gun in her hand...

Idly, Kate wondered why the interest in the possibility of a Stepford wife in their midst, but everyone was busy ignoring the fact that a Three Families mother headed up an international drug business. Maybe it was that with the explanation came instant recognition of all Mum Hamilton had hidden over the years. She'd hidden it well, but now they knew about it no one was surprised. Or maybe being a drug lord came second to being a submissive wife. Or maybe it was because she still had a gun in her hand...

"She's leaving with her lover," Kate muttered. "Her lover?" She looked towards the doorway in which Mum

176

Hamilton and Weasel-Face still lingered as if reluctant to finally depart. Weasel-Face was her lover? Weasel-Face? Surely not! But there appeared to be no other contender for that position so she had to assume that Weasel-Face was indeed Mum Hamilton's lover.

It took all sorts... Just as well they didn't all have the same taste or there'd be no Zorro for anyone. Not that she was in to Zorro any more. Oh, no. She'd grown out of that youthful, hero-obsessed folly at least an hour ago.

To try not to think of it, Kate considered Errol instead, currently moaning while he lay on the floor with a leg wound given him by his mother for tricking her. That had shown more gumption than she'd thought he possessed. In fact, Kate realised, it had been clever of him to pretend to pick up poo to search for a chip in it. It made Mum Hamilton feel secure when she shouldn't have, and directly led to her confessing that the essential information required to keep her drug business going was indeed on the chip.

Kate knew that someone had been picking up Jeff-Dog's poo, though, and going to some lengths to get their hands on it, but she wasn't going to worry about that just now. She had a suspicion that might have been Errol, but she didn't blame him for covering all bases just in case there *was* a chip in the poo...

"Makes no difference," Mum Hamilton said as Weasel-Face disappeared through the door and she turned to follow him. "You don't really believe I'd only make one copy of all that info do you? You might have the main chip but you don't have all the info. The business can still carry on with or without that chip."

The main chip? There really had been a chip? Implanted in her lovely dog without permission! Finally, it was making sense to her and she didn't want to look at her poor used and abused dog who currently demonstrated his magnanimity of spirit by licking enthusiastically at Errol's ankle where his trouser leg had rucked up while he writhed in agony on the floor. He bore him no ill-will at all for pinching his poo.

"You're not nearly as bright as you think," Dad Hamilton said to his wife. "It makes no difference how many copies there are. As we speak, and as you waste time arguing with me when you should be getting away, all the scum on that chip are being picked up by vice. Headed up, just by the way, by our own Pete Benning, who's been in on the whole show from the word go, it turns out. He's an undercover disgraced cop."

Mum Hamilton hissed.

"Oh, you thought you really had him with those bribes? Nope. He's been undercover all along. You know – *pretending* to be a corrupt cop."

Kate wondered if her dad had known this. No, surely not. Nor her mother. Pete might have put on a brilliant show and done a courageous thing, but he wasn't half in trouble with Stella now! The relief that he wasn't bent was more than she expected. She had to bite her lip hard to stop it trembling and make sure she didn't blink for as long as possible in the hope the tears dried up before they fell.

Mum Hamilton disappeared from the doorway.

Shortly afterwards, the keening wail of sirens filled the night air and the tension in the room eased.

Finally able to bring herself to face her dog, Kate carefully rolled back and removed his so recently restored balaclava and gingerly felt through the thick fur around his neck. She found where a flap of skin had been cut and then stitched again. Presumably this was where the chip had been stored. If Dad Hamilton wasn't one of the foremost surgeons in the UK she would be having words with him. She might have words with him anyway. He could have asked before kidnapping and carving her dog up. At least Jeff-Dog didn't seem bothered by his experience. If he'd been at all traumatised she'd have been furious.

"It's all right," Dad Hamilton said. "A tiny amount of local anaesthetic and it took seconds to remove. Even getting it in there, Mum Hamilton used a type of injecting kit. He won't have felt a thing."

"Hmphh!" Kate didn't know how to feel about her dog being used so blatantly as a carrier of drug information. Did that make him some kind of mule?

"Think of it this way – if he'd fallen into the hands of the other lot he probably wouldn't have been treated nearly so well. I took it out for his own good. It can be read in situ actually, but if it had been left in him he would always have been a target."

Kate bent over and hugged Jeff-Dog, but he was too busy saying an excited hello to his surgeon to take much notice of her. He was far too forgiving, that dog!

Chapter Twenty-three

"Actually, I'm bluffing and she's probably lying, but it makes no difference to me anyway," Dad Hamilton said. "My children are my children whoever the sperm donor might be."

Kate turned back to him. Jeff-Dog had said hello to her again and had moved on to fresh prey. There were many willing recipients of his affection and he was going to make the most of it. As long as he was safe, that was all she could get her head around for the time being.

All the rest of the fallout was like a movie being played around her. She was quite impressed with Dad Hamilton, though. She'd never particularly noticed him as an individual before. How strange that one's view of someone could change so radically so quickly.

"What I don't get," she said. "Is that some people knew some stuff that other people didn't. This has obviously been some kind of conspiracy where some people set out to get Mum Hamilton and the Counters, including her children. This must have included Pete pretending to be a corrupt cop, and some people knew he was doing that and some didn't. It seems that different members of The Three Families knew different amounts of stuff."

Mum and Dad Cole smiled encouragingly at her from where they sat, but no one said anything.

She glanced at Tom. He'd been moving around the room all this time and she had the feeling he'd been readying himself to leap in the way of any bullets that might have been directed at her. Something about his face caught her attention.

It took a moment to work it out. When she did she didn't understand it. Tom looked more carefree than he'd looked for months. He looked like he used to look before he got all possessive and clingy.

"And some of us knew nothing at all," Kate muttered to herself. "Some of us were just getting on with our lives and knew nothing at all." She clapped her hands to her face. She couldn't believe she'd been quite so unaware of all the shenanigans going on around her involving her family and closest friends. But it was beginning to percolate through to her that Tom had known all along and he'd wanted to keep her unaware but also he'd wanted to keep her safe. And she'd been so mean to him...

Still! It served him right. He should have told her instead of trying to protect her. Regardless of the logic behind this, she still felt mean and she gave him a small smile which felt more like she was baring her teeth at him so she stopped doing it and, looking around for a distraction, realised she couldn't see Jeff-Dog anymore.

She checked all around the room. There was no sign that a dog had ever been in it. And then she spotted the door was open...

"Where's Jeff-Dog?" she shrieked in sudden panic, wildly staring at where he was not to be seen. One minute he was there, the next minute he was gone.

"Bugger!" Errol said. "There'll be other Counters around who think the chip's still in the dog. Wisley put out a reward last night. I kept bumping into some of them while following you around, Kate."

Errol was sitting at the kitchen table with his father kneeling on the floor in front of him putting the finishing touches to his bandaged leg. As Dad Hamilton stood up and eyed his handiwork with some satisfaction, Errol continued: "But it's only a dog. We can get you another one."

Tom shot across the room and grabbed Errol by his sweatshirt, bunching it up in fistfuls. But Kate knew he'd not hit him, not with a leg wound. This was far too noble and Zorro-like for her satisfaction and she therefore felt obliged to follow him over to Errol and kick him in the leg. She managed to stop herself kicking his injured one, but he still

181

bellowed as if she had, and doubled over while Tom looked at her reproachfully as if she'd let the side down. She was unrepentant and not in the least bit interested in all that high-principled stuff, not when her dog was missing. Again.

"My dog," she addressed Errol, "is not a commodity that can be replaced merely by getting another one. Don't speak to me ever again until you understand that."

She knew that was unlikely to happen in her lifetime.

By this time Tom had dropped Errol back in his chair and disappeared. Kate could hear running footsteps, shouting, the gunning of a car engine and wildly excited dog barks. She ran after him and was just in time to see Tom leap athletically at a car that was moving off.

Risking dismemberment, he somehow got his arm into the gap as the back door was closing and wrenched it open again. He then fell over backwards as the momentum of the car pulled him off his feet. But it was enough. Jeff-Dog leapt from the car barking madly, wagging his tail furiously, absolutely delighted with life. The car zoomed off and Jeff-Dog fell on Tom who tried to fend off his enthusiastic greetings, but failed. He gave up and the dog lay full length on him and licked his face clean.

Kate came running up and without pausing to consider she kicked Tom in the leg. He and Jeff-Dog immediately shot to their feet; Tom scowling; Jeff-Dog ready for action.

"What was that for?" Tom demanded, rubbing the place where there'd be a huge bruise tomorrow.

"I was just making sure you were okay," she yelled, puzzled at her own fury but too frightened to rein it in. "You could have been killed or seriously injured. What were you thinking?"

"I was thinking Jeff-Dog needed to be got away from the Counters who would have carved him up to get the chip they thought was still in him."

The screeching sound of a car leaving most of its tyres on the tarmac filled the air and they turned towards the end of the road in time to see the nearly-gotaway-with-Jeff-

Dog vehicle blocked from exiting the street by a posse of police vans. Counters leapt out of their car and tried to run for freedom, shouts and curses filled the night air, accompanied by the odd firework, and it was all over in not much time.

"Well, I didn't know they would be picked up quite so soon or I'd have left it to them," Tom added a mite testily.

"They might not have been if you hadn't delayed them by that amount of time. Good job, too. I didn't think Mum Hamilton should get away. I am very grateful to you, Tom," Kate said. "And so is Jeff-Dog – between here and there," she gestured to the end of the terrace, "They could have carved him up. If you had left it to them he might already be a goner." She smiled at him, but she could tell by his slightly uneasy answering smile that he was very confused about whether she really wanted to kick him or hug him.

As she wasn't too sure herself, she was pleased when Pete approached to say that they were headed back to 'the ranch' now.

Back to the ranch? For a moment Kate felt as if she were nine again, without a care in the world when The Three Families were whole and uncorrupted. Well, as far as she knew anyway...

"I have to tell Mum before anyone else does," Pete added, an apprehensive look on his face that Kate totally understood! She wouldn't want to be in his shoes when Stella found out about the deception that had been played on her, whether 'in the line of duty' or not...

It was with some relief that she climbed into the SUV, Jeff-Dog by her side, switched on the ignition and drove off into the night, heading for home. When she pulled up outside her parents' house she was startled to discover she had a car full of people. She hadn't even noticed them getting in to the vehicle. She had the same passengers she'd had on the outward trip, minus Spencer and Errol, plus Mum Cole who was squashed into the back with Dad Cole as though they'd never be apart again. Mum Cole had a curiously satisfied look on her face as if things were going her way.

They piled out at House Benning to find that Pete and Dad Hamilton had got there first, and were helping Errol up the path towards the open front door. A white-faced Stella Benning stood waiting for them.

Kate's relief at not being the one in the line of fire was so great she thought her knees were going to melt.

Chapter Twenty-four

Sitting on a bench in the garden idly watching fireworks light up the night sky Kate tried to get her thoughts in order, but she knew she was missing some essential information.

Without prompting, Tom spoke out of the gloom: "I knew that Spencer was embezzling funds from the business. I didn't know why, but I did know he was doing it in such a ham-fisted way that he wanted to be caught. I thought he was asking for attention so I tackled him about it and he confessed to losing a lot of money gambling. He'd had this problem before and successfully overcome it, but he'd relapsed. It's something he'll always have to watch out for but he's especially prone to it if stressed."

"Why didn't he just ask you to help him out?" Kate wanted to know. "You're supposed to be best friends, after all."

"He'd gone to his mother. At that point he didn't know she was a criminal. He really didn't. She paid off his debts. They were held by someone pretty nasty, I gather. She – Mum Hamilton – had been wanting to get Spencer into her 'business' for a long time. She wanted her own private accountant looking after her books. But it was only after he went to her about the gambling that she could see how to make him join her. She threatened trouble for his father and for his friends. That's us. She wanted him to embezzle the firm to show he had a greater allegiance to her than to me to prove she could trust him. He was in a very difficult situation. The only thing he could think to do was make a mess of the embezzling so he'd be caught. Also, if he'd involved me directly I'd have been in greater danger from the Counters. He was trying to avoid that."

185

"So – why are they called 'Counters'?"

"I think she was originally called 'The Counter' because she was always counting her ill-gotten gains. It became a general term for all of them in that 'gang'. She's sometimes called 'Countess' now as well."

Kate was struck by a sudden thought. "How long ago did you find out?" she asked.

"Two or three months ago," Tom said. He rubbed his eyes and Kate looked at him properly for the first time for... two or three months.

He looked so tired! And he looked so tired because he'd been watching out for her – he'd been 'keeping an eye out' for her! The sudden revelation with its accompanying uprush of feeling made her punch him in the arm. She was horrified at her reaction. She'd so recently kicked him and now she'd punched him as well. It was too late to take it back, though.

"Ow!" he shouted, clutching his afflicted limb. "What did you do that for?"

"Because, you idiot – you've been guarding me haven't you? You haven't been spying on me or being insanely possessive or stalking me – you've been keeping me safe, haven't you?" He didn't even have to answer. She knew the truth of it as surely as she knew her own shoe size.

"And this makes me an idiot?" he queried, his voice stiff with hurt.

"It does when you make me think you're getting all horribly possessive and I've just become a thing you own! Why didn't you tell me?"

"You'd have been in even greater danger if I'd told you. And that's apart from what you'd have done. You're hopelessly impulsive about some things."

He was going to make her cross again at this rate. Kate concentrated on the thought that he'd been keeping her safe all this time. No wonder he looked so exhausted. And she'd rewarded him by breaking off their engagement and being horrible to him. Trouble is, there wasn't much she could do about it now. It was too late. The misunderstanding had gone too deep and she was in love with another now – in love with a swashbuckling, cape-swirling, black-clad hero. Oh, yes! She looked around as if he'd appear, but he didn't.

She sighed. All she could see in the heavy gloom was random white flashes as Jeff-Dog scurried through the undergrowth chasing adventure. And she was glad because she'd gone off Zorro as well. He'd turned out to be an illusion and it was time she faced life as it was rather than as she imagined it should be. It was time she grew up and looked beyond the next pot of compost filled with hopeful seedlings.

And anyway – he'd probably gallop off with someone else behind him in the saddle when he knew she wasn't prepared to leave her dog behind.

She sighed again. Heavily and loudly and lengthily. Tom got up without a word and went back into the house.

Chapter Twenty-five

Getting cold, but strangely reluctant to rejoin the company, it was a while before Kate and Jeff-Dog entered the kitchen; Jeff-Dog immediately slid under the table, lay down with a thump that forced the air out of his lungs with a whoosh, and rested his head on Tom's foot. Kate sat down opposite Tom. Tom didn't look up. He appeared to be studying the grain of the wooden table top – studying it as if it would give him the answers to the most important questions in his life.

Maybe it would. Kate imagined that he might feel as though none of the people around him were making any sense. His lifelong friend, who happened to be his fiancée, too, had broken off their engagement, and done it publicly. His best friend and business partner had swindled him and then made off with his father's money without a backward glance. His father might have had an affair with a drug baroness and his mother had moved out of the family home to teach her husband a lesson about complacency.

Tom looked so isolated where he sat. Kate's heart squinched up in sympathy.

She could hear voices rising and falling from the next room. No doubt Stella was putting Pete through a wringer about being undercover and not telling her; about leading her to believe – not that she had believed it – that he was a corrupt cop. Kate didn't envy him at all and wondered if she should go and support him, but she might make things worse.

Anyway, she had things to sort out here.

"About Spencer," Kate said, and saw Tom stiffen slightly, but otherwise not react in any way at all. "You let him get away, didn't you?"

No answer was forthcoming.

Kate slid her hand across the table and lightly clasped one of his. "In fact, the whole thing was a set-up wasn't it – you not only let him get away but somehow you arranged for him to have the money to do it. Your father's money. So Dad Cole must also have been in on it." Tom's hand quivered and stilled, but he made no reply.

"I don't get the bit about Mum Cole being kidnapped, though. How did that fit in?"

Finally, Tom looked up. "It wasn't supposed to be Mum Cole," he said. "It was supposed to be Bridget that was so-say kidnapped. So that she could go with Spencer when he left."

"Bridget?" Kate couldn't believe what she was hearing.

Seriously? Spencer and Tom were such romantics they believed Bridget would want to live a life on the run with no guarantee of luxury. She didn't have the heart to say anything, thereby completely murdering any sliver of romanticism there might be left in Tom's psyche.

"Of course, Bridget," Tom said, a trifle impatiently. "She is, or she was, Spencer's fiancée. She'd have wanted to go with him wherever he went. Or that's what we thought. We hadn't anticipated she be quite as fickle as she turned out to be."

Kate could think of nothing to say. What planet were these men living on? She merely held his hand a little tighter while thoughts of masked rescuers flickered on the edge of her mind. Maybe it was a childish thing, this hero-obsession. Maybe she should forget about flowing capes and heroes riding off with her into the dawn. Maybe that was what she should have dreamed of in her teens rather than now...

Poor Tom. All his disillusions were coming home to roost in one crowded, motley go!

"So, what was all that about Dad Cole and Mum Hamilton supposedly having an affair? I don't get it."

Kate frowned at their hands clasped on the kitchen table. The people those hands belonged to might as well be on separate continents. She felt as if she was trying to plough a field with a teaspoon.

"No, nor me," Tom said. "We'll have to ask them."

But he said it in such a heavy tone of voice Kate knew he didn't want to ask them, in case there were any more secrets he didn't want to hear.

Kate knew she needed to leave now before she threw herself on him out of gut-wrenching sympathy. He looked so woeful.

But she didn't want to mislead him so she patted his hand and got up to leave. Jeff-Dog's claws clicked on the floor behind her.

Chapter Twenty-six

Kate knocked loudly on what had so recently been Bridget's front door. She wasn't taking a closed door for an answer, and she wanted answers now. Mum Cole would give them to her. Oh, yes!

Jeff-Dog, his tail slowly swaying from side to side in anticipation, stuck his nose on the door and snuffled energetically as if he could snort a hole through the wood. As she watched, Kate saw his tail speed up until it was a blur. She stepped back as the door opened to show Mum Cole wrapped in a flimsy negligee of Bridget's, her hands protectively holding it closed. Kate had seen this set before and admired it although she knew she wouldn't have the confidence to wear it herself. The long nightdress was the ethereal green of new beech leaves with a lovely coppery lacy shaping over the bust. A diaphanous negligee with the same laciness on the sleeves didn't do much to cover the form beneath.

"You look amazing!" Kate exclaimed, grinning widely at Mum Cole and hoping she hadn't sounded as surprised as she felt.

"I was just trying on a few things," Mum Cole said, flushing, unable to look directly at Kate. "I wanted to know what it felt like to wear sexy clothes. I'm not sure it's me..."

"I don't see why not! I think you should practice with Bridget's wardrobe and then get your own stuff and seduce Dad Cole. Why not?"

Mum Cole's colour heightened. Wordlessly, she stepped back welcoming Kate and Jeff-Dog into her new home. She then made a complete mockery of her sexy outfit by busily setting about making hot chocolate. Kate sat at the table and looked forward to it. No one had ever made hot chocolate like Mum Cole did. Nowhere else in all the world had she found hot chocolate as creamy and yummy as Mum Cole's, and yet not too horribly sweet.

Finally, they were both settled with Jeff-Dog taking up his usual position under the table.

Mum Cole straightened her coaster, obviously taking her time whilst formulating what she would say; she studied Kate's coaster, too, and tentatively reached out as if to straighten that one as well, before her hand retreated back to fiddle with the handle of her mug.

Pulling in a deep breath and finally looking up at her unexpected late-night guest she said: "Kate, I'm sorry I deceived you, but I had to. We were trying to protect Bridget. Tom wanted to get Spencer away so he could start a new life. Even though he betrayed their friendship and misappropriated funds from the business, Tom didn't want Spencer to get caught up in all the drug stuff."

"Tom said Spencer's swindling was so clumsy it was more a call for attention than anything else," Kate said.

"Yes. We believe he was deliberately being slipshod so that Tom would discover it. Spencer was in so deep with the Counters that he couldn't refuse them, or not without endangering himself and Bridget. They were blackmailing him," she added in answer to Kate's unspoken query. "He had nothing to do with the drug operation. Gambling was his downfall and they used that against him."

Kate leaned over the table and took her hand.

"And, yes," Mum Cole continued. "I do think that Bridget's incessant and escalating demands might have helped push Spencer into his gambling, but it wouldn't have been a problem if he hadn't already had a problem."

"I agree. Bridget can be a little self-centred, but it's not her fault that Spencer turned to the horses, or whatever."

Mum Cole smiled gratefully at her and they both let go of each other and grabbed their mugs. Silence reigned for a while except for Jeff-Dog's snuffling under the table where he was busy hoovering up anything that lay around, edible or otherwise.

"So..." Kate said, wrinkling her brow, trying to round up all the loose ends in her mind. "The money. Two hundred thousand pounds is a lot of cash to just have lying about the place."

"Yes. And of course, it wasn't just lying about the place. It was the amount we decided would give Spencer a fair chance to disappear and start a new life."

"It's very generous," Kate said.

"What price friendship?" Mum Cole said. "Tom was desperate for Spencer to have a chance. Even so, he's lost his best friend. They were more than friends. They were true brothers in spirit for their entire lives. And now they're lost to each other. It's very sad."

Kate was conscious that Tom had lost his business, his best friend *and* his fiancée in one fell swoop and was grateful that Mum Cole didn't labour the point.

"So you knew that Bridget was to be kidnapped... No! Wait! You set the whole thing up, of course! That's how Spencer would get the money. Why didn't you just give it to him? It would have been a lot easier and without the risks."

"It certainly would have been easier, but Tom wouldn't have it. He wanted Spencer to have the money but he wanted him to take responsibility for it so that Dad Cole couldn't possibly be accused of helping a criminal escape. Hence the kidnap farce. Also, of course, it was meant to be Bridget so they'd leave together."

Kate nodded. Yes, that made sense. Except for the idea that Bridget would have gone along with it... "But what about..." she began, only to be rudely interrupted by someone banging on the door. Jeff-Dog flew out from under the table and barked wildly at the presence outside. Kate and Mum Cole looked at each other. Who on earth could it be at this time of night?

A shrill voice soon let them know. "Let me in! It's my flat. You have no right to keep me out of my own flat!"

Bridget. Of course.

Mum Cole shrugged and Kate got up to answer the door. Upon opening it she found herself pushed unceremoniously out of the way as Bridget barged through closely followed by Weasel-Face who slammed the door shut and squared up to the three of them, a truculent sneer enhancing his weasel-features.

Jeff-Dog, protector-extraordinaire, hurled himself forward. Weasel-Face flinched and flattened his body against the door only to find himself beleaguered by a dog wanting to say an enthusiastic hello; jumping up with little yelps of joy, aiming his tongue at his weaselly face.

Traitor-dog!

"Why did you let him in?" Kate demanded of Bridget.

"He was hanging around outside. Reckons you owe him some money. Anyway, I'm here to get my life back so I'll ask you all to leave."

No one moved.

"Okay. I'm demanding you all leave. Now," Kate said.

"You're not in a position to demand anything, love," Weasel said. "I'm the one demanding something and I'm demanding the dosh. I want this two hundred kay everyone keeps going on about."

"Two hundred kay? What are you on about?" Mum Cole said, scorn rife in her voice.

"He means two hundred thousand pounds, Mum," Bridget kindly explained, contempt rife in hers.

Kate nearly laughed but managed to restrain herself.

"Yes, dear. I did manage to work that out. But what two hundred thousand pounds exactly is he talking about?"

Bridget said nothing.

"Well? Cat got your tongue?" Mum Cole said to her daughter much to Kate's shock. Mum Cole would never have talked to anyone like that before. Maybe this was all part of her transformation. Kate really hoped the new Mum Cole would still find it in her heart to make her fruitilicious ice lollies!

Bridget was apparently just as shocked and merely stared at her mother as if wondering where the rightful Mum Cole had gone.

"The two hundred kay yer hubby was going to pay to get you back!" Weasel said.

"No. Nope. Drawing a blank here," Mum Cole said staring at him, a look of such complete innocence on her face she absolutely had to be lying through her teeth.

"Now, look here!" Weasel began stepping to the side to get past Jeff-Dog. He was foiled in that Jeff-Dog jumped to the side, too, and when Weasel stepped back again so did Jeff-Dog.

What a good dog! He was protecting them after all. He was managing to do it whilst looking like he wasn't actually doing it. What a clever dog!

"And, anyway, I don't believe there ever really was two hundred kay," Bridget said. "Dad refused point blank to pay for a raft of white doves to be released at my wedding. If he really had that much money lying around why would he do that?" She looked around the assembled company as if for acknowledgement of a salient point well-made.

Mum Cole and Kate looked at each other, their faces so blank Kate thought they could safely take up poker if they ever found themselves broke on a riverboat.

Weasel-Face stared at Bridget as though he'd never seen anything like it before in his life. "A raft of white doves? A raft?" he said. "Get it right ferfricksake. It's doves innit! It has to be a bevy or a flight or, most appropriately if it's for a wedding, it's a piteousness or a pitying of doves."

He stopped as he realized everyone, even Jeff-Dog, was staring at him, their mouths open.

"Well, before I got in with the Counters I was looking around for a business, see," he said. "Gotta earn a living, you know. One way or another. Yeah. I looked at specializing in dove release for weddings and stuff. You know, they say if doves are seen at a wedding the happy couple will be together forever. Yeah. They do. You train them, see, to spread their wings, fly up into the sky and then they circle together a bit before flying home. It's symbolic of the bride and groom blooming and growing and starting a new life together. Lovely, it is. Yeah."

He looked dreamily around the room as if seeing it all before him. Kate had no such picture in her usually well over-active and colourful mind. Weasel-Face seemed the most inappropriate person to spread joy with a load of pitying doves! But then, it takes all sorts...

"The pair of you have no appreciation of living things. How do you think the doves feel? They're kept in tiny cages." Mum Cole said.

Weasel-Face avoided the accusation. "Well, anyway, I didn't do it. Got in with the Counters instead."

"The counters?" Bridget said. "Honestly, I haven't the faintest idea what any of you are on about. Talking of which," she turned to her mother. "What's all this about Dad having it off with Mum Hamilton?"

"He wasn't!" Weasel-Face shouted, going puce so suddenly Kate really hoped he wasn't going to keel over, although that would be an answer to their current predicament...

"I can't imagine it," Bridget nodded in agreement with him. "They're too old for a start. Ooh..." She shuddered.

"She's not too old!" Weasel-Face shouted.

"No, she's not," Mum Cole said. "Neither's my husband. But they weren't having an affair."

"Why did Mum Hamilton go along with it, then, when you both said they were having an affair?" Kate wanted to know.

"You can always rely on her to cause trouble if she doesn't have to actually go to any trouble herself to do it," Mum Cole said, a tad bitterly. "They did have Clark between them. That part's true."

"That was a long time ago, though," Kate said.

They looked up, startled, as Weasel-Face suddenly clapped his hands to his head. "What am I doing?" he yelled to the night. "What am I doing? I want the dosh. I'm here to get the dosh. Where's the two hundred kay? Stop distracting me with talk of rafts and old lovers and stuff and give me the dosh!"

"If there is any such dosh you're sure as hell not getting it!" Bridget declared. "If anyone's getting it, it'll be me for all the inconvenience I've been put to tonight. And then I can have my raft of doves."

Weasel-Face stared at her and muttered: "Raft..." He turned to Mum Cole and shook his head. "Maybe you deserve it," he said. "To put up with that. There never was two hundred kay was there. I thought it was worth checking though. That'd have been a nice, tidy sum to take with us. My sweetie's got enough dosh, but I'd have liked some of my own."

"It would hardly have been yours if you'd stolen it from us, would it?" Kate snapped.

"Of course it would! If I'd stolen it from you, it *would* be mine. That's the whole point of stealing."

"Well, that's me told," Kate muttered.

"You're all bonkers, you lot," Weasel-Face said in disgust. "I'm off before I catch anything from you." And he was gone, much to Jeff-Dog's dismay and everyone else's delight.

It was as if he hadn't yet realised his 'sweetie' had already been taken into custody, Kate thought.

"What was all that about?" Bridget demanded, immediately going on: "No. Don't tell me. I'm not really interested. Just being polite. Can we get back to me now?"

Mum Cole and Kate exchanged another look and Mum Cole opened her mouth, but before she could say anything the door was thrust open so hard it slammed against the wall and bounced back again, but the figure that appeared in the doorway was ready for it and caught it before it smacked into him. It was Zorro.

All in black, including black suede shoes; his ensemble completed by his balaclava. He stood silently regarding them. They gazed back at him. It was difficult to see him in the shadows which shifted with the movement of

197

the trees outside as the moon poured its light through their branches and in through the landing window.

"My work here is done," he whispered.

Always with the bloody whispering! Kate thought savagely.

"And I'm away," Zorro continued. "But I will be back if I'm needed." Briefly he looked each of the three women directly in the eyes.

And then he was gone.

What was that about? Kate wondered. And why did he look so significantly at each of them in turn? A sudden thought crashed through her mind and she gasped, immediately turning it into a cough to cover herself.

He wasn't her Zorro! He was everyone's Zorro! He'd appeared to them all! What a sod! What a philandering unfaithful fickle sod!

She turned to the other two and saw that Bridget had a dreamy look on her face. Her hands were clasped together over her heart in typical maiden-waiting-to-be-rescued pose. Mum Cole looked almost as smitten. Kate decided to say nothing. Why squash someone else's fantasy?

But when she turned back to the doorway again there was another Zorro. She knew it wasn't the same one by his shoes. These shoes were also black, but shiny.

So maybe they'd each had their own Zorro?

This one didn't say anything and was only there fleetingly. Kate didn't think Bridget or Mum Cole had even seen him. He put his finger to his lips when he saw her looking at him, and then he disappeared too.

"It's all very well for you, Kate! Sitting there with that scornful look on your face," Bridget said. "You've always had your own Batman. You've had him your whole life. You've always complained about him looking after you, looking out for you, keeping an eye on you, guarding you. Moaned on and on about him being too possessive and stalking you. It's every girl's dream to have someone like that."

Kate kept her poker face on. No way was it every girl's dream to have to deal with that kind of insane possessiveness and paranoia. What Bridget didn't know was that finally Kate realized it wasn't that at all. He'd been looking out for her out of a real fear that the criminals who'd encroached on her life recently without her being at all aware of them might harm her. She could have cried. He had been really protecting her even at great personal cost to himself because he knew she hated being so crowded by him.

"He's spent his whole life waiting for you to really see him," Bridget continued. "The rest of us have to make do with crumbs, with glimpses of people in fancy dress at New Year's." Bridget sounded positively sulky.

"Batman?" Kate said at the same time as Mum Cole queried: "Fancy dress?"

They both stared at Bridget.

Bridget stared back. "Du...uh... He was dressed as Batman. Obviously!"

Kate and Mum Cole continued to stare. Kate could think of nothing sensible to say.

"Bat...man..." Bridget said very, very slowly. Her audience was obviously a bit thick. "All in black with a mask on." She waited a few seconds and shook her head. "I despair," she muttered.

"Well, go and despair in your own home," Mum Cole said.

"This *is* my home!" Bridget said.

"No, it's not. It's mine now. Your home is with your father."

"No! You can't mean that! You've had your fun. Now let's all get back to normal."

"No. I don't think so. Your normal isn't good enough. Neither is mine. This way we can both grow up a bit. And so can your father."

As if on cue a third Zorro filled the doorway. Kate was pretty sure she heard Mum Cole whisper: "My Scarlet Pimpernel," as this black-clad figure whipped off his balaclava to reveal Dad Cole grinning like a boy, clearly chuffed with himself.

Mum Cole fluttered and simpered and Kate could see the Coles' courtship was getting off to a flying start. It was time to get out of here!

She made for the door dragging Bridget with her, Jeff-Dog scurrying along behind.

Even so, she noted with some surprise that Bridget ran back to her parents and gave them quick hugs before racing after Kate.

"I'll pick Bridget up from you in ten minutes," Dad Cole called after them.

"Anyone would think I was a bit of luggage," Bridget said bitterly as she trailed along with Kate to her part of the house. "No one wants me. At least someone wants you. Even if you don't want him."

Kate wasn't sure what to say. It seemed mean to rub salt in the wound, but Bridget had dumped Spencer so many times over the years. Often publicly. She couldn't really wallow in a trough of despondency and expect sympathy now. It was confusing to know who had dumped whom half the time...

Waiting for Dad Cole to come for Bridget, Kate watched the first glimmer of light steal its way across the night sky. Looking down from her window it was still too dark to make anything out in the back garden, but in the utter stillness of approaching dawn she became conscious of a rhythmic drumming that sounded uncannily like hooves. She looked back into the room, but Jeff-Dog was quietly minding his own business chewing his paw.

Bridget stood immobile as if she, too, listened.

Kate, struck by the intensity of her friend's most-unBridgetlike-concentration, involuntarily stepped towards her, but before she reached her Bridget moved her way instead and hugged her hard. Stepping back she gave Kate a somewhat tremulous smile.

"Forgive me, Kate, for the deceptions. We had to do it like this to make sure we could get away together, or someone would have stopped us. Spencer *is* my superhero. He *is* my Batman. And we're going to live happily ever after. I do love everyone. Don't let them forget that. And I so wish you find your hero, too."

And she disappeared through the doorway. Kate heard her running lightly down the stairs, the outer door opened and shut and she was gone.

Back at the window, the night had lightened enough to make out the deep black silhouette of a horseman galloping across the lawn. A slim figure, hair and dress flowing, ran towards him, arms outstretched.

Kate saw the rider lean down towards Bridget and grasp her about the waist as if the two of them had been practising circus routines their whole lives. Bridget landed in the saddle in front of the rider and leaned back against him as if she'd never move from that position again.

Both figures raised an arm and waved. They knew she'd be watching. She waved back even though they wouldn't see it. Suddenly, she was overwhelmed with sobs. Tears flooded down her face as she watched them canter away. She had no idea why she was crying. Jeff-Dog was puzzled, too, and repeatedly pushed his nose into her leg until she sat on the floor with him, her arms around his neck, her face pressed into his biscuity-smelling fur.

Chapter Twenty-seven

When she again heard the rhythmic drumming of hooves her heart sank. Either Spencer and Bridget had forgotten something and were coming back for it, risking getting caught, or they were running away from pursuers who'd lain in wait for them.

Or it was her own Zorro this time.

With the heavily star-speckled and dawn-streaked sky behind him Kate could clearly see Zorro galloping along on his horse, his cape flying out behind him, his hat – the proper kind of hat for a Zorro – clearly delineated against the indigo of the heavens.

She knew her heart should have been leaping into her throat in that way it always does in the best romances at this point, but somehow it wasn't doing that at all. In fact, her heart was weighing her down. It was heavy and unsettled and full of regret. Jeff-Dog's head bumped against her leg because he knew she needed to take comfort from its warmth and silkiness.

Now what was she going to do?

She already knew what she was going to do, but, oh, how hard was it going to be?

By now she and her trusty hound had exited the house and stood at the edge of the lawn. Zorro approached her across the previously immaculate sward, no doubt now pockmarked with hoofprints.

Up close to her Zorro's horse whickered softly as if to say: "We're here for you." Kate peered through the night but couldn't see Zorro's face and he said nothing. The four of them stood there quietly for a while as if being content in each other's company would be enough for ever.

Now. She had to do it now. She had to tell him she had her own hero already and she didn't want Zorro. Not this Zorro anyway. Not any more.

She was very grateful for all he'd done for her over the last day or so, especially getting Jeff-Dog from the House of Hell for her. But he wasn't the hero for her.

There was another hero she wanted.

Kate and Jeff-Dog leapt back yelping as a voice from a quite different direction to the one expected, spoke in her ear: "I hired all the correct gear," the voice said. "It's amazing what you can get even on New Year's Eve. Look, see the black, flowing Spanish cape, the proper domino mask and the real sombrero-cordobés hat. Then there's the horse. Completely black, as it should be."

He paused for breath. Kate and Jeff-Dog stared at him as if they'd never seen him before. He continued: "Of course, I was going to ride in on the horse, as all good Zorros should. But then I thought, what do I do with the dog? Will he ride on the back of the saddle? Will he follow the horse? What if he can't keep up? What if he gets too exhausted chasing along after a galloping horse? What if the horse kicks him? That wouldn't go down very well with my Kate, I thought. It was a dilemma. I'm not even going to mention my utter terror at the very idea of getting on a horse. Especially one that size. It's the size of a... well – a very big, tall, enormous horse..."

Kate opened her mouth but shut it again as Tom reached for her hand and inspected it closely. He seldom spoke so fast and breathlessly and she could only assume he was, for some reason, nervous. It was interesting, though. She was happy to let him blather on except now she was conscious of someone on a horse listening in, too. Who the hell was that?

"It's curious that my ring is still on your finger," Tom said, poking it. "When I gave it to you it was too big and we were going to get it altered, but we never did. So why can't you get it off? Have you got fat? Have you got so fat you can't get the ring off? If you have, I hadn't noticed. You're perfect just the way you are so if you have got fat I'm happy with that." He poked the ring again, looked at her and away again. "I shouldn't have said that, should I? About you getting fat, but if you have…"

"Don't say it again! It's fine, but you don't need to say it again. I haven't got fat. Um – could we dispense with the audience, do you think?" Kate asked trying to subtly gesture with her head to the horseman behind them.

Tom looked up surprised as if he'd forgotten the redundant Zorro. "Yes! Of course." He turned to the black-clad figure. "Thanks ever so much, Fred. Don't forget to bring your accounts in. We have a special, low-cost scheme for small-business accounting."

"Great, mate. I'll see you soon, then. Happy New Year!" And he galloped off.

"It's very odd about not being able to get the ring off, then," Tom said as if dispensing with the services of a Zorro-for-hire called Fred was a commonplace thing unworthy of mention.

Kate followed his lead. "I *can* get the ring off." She removed her hand from his grasp and pulled at the ring. It slid easily from her finger and she held it up to sparkle in the first fires of dawn. "I can get the ring off, but I can't *leave* it off. My finger feels naked without it. My finger feels wrong without it. So I can take it off, but I can't leave it off, so I can't really take it off."

"That is odd…"

"Not really. I could always get it off, but when I tried to take it off I knew I didn't want to. It had to stay right where it was until it was ready, and it simply hasn't ever been ready. Even when I really wanted to take it off before going into the Badlands I just couldn't make myself do it."

"Even at dinner during confessions and confections – you were struggling with it then."

"I didn't want to take it off," she agreed. "Simple, really. Nothing felt right without it on my finger."

"So you could actually take it off, but you didn't want to…" he said slowly as if he had to carefully work through the complexities of this.

"Maybe it's because we've been engaged in my mind for my whole life? Maybe it's because I'm so wrapped up in my compost and bits of twig that I'm incapable of thinking of life being different to the way I've always thought it?"

"You're not going to let me forget that, are you?"

"Nope."

"What I do want you to forget is us being engaged," Tom said.

Kate drew away from him, shock rattling in her chest.

"I'm not a decent proposition for you now. The ring will come off when it's ready. I understand you felt crowded by me and I'm sorry. I just wanted you to be safe. You were the one who didn't know anything at all about what was going on and I was terrified you'd be harmed somehow. But now that we've got Spencer safely away to a new life I need to get my business back on track. It's in tatters now. And Dad's too. I feel responsible."

"You want me to forget about us being engaged because of the money that Spencer embezzled, and because of the two hundred kay?"

"It's a lot of money to lose. It means I can't provide for you the way I should."

"See, now there it is. You don't need to provide for me, thank you. Maybe provide for us, but not just for me. And anyway, maybe I can provide for you instead. Maybe I can provide for us. These twigs and things are doing quite nicely, you know."

"I know."

"You do?"

"Uh – we *are* your accountants…"

"Oh, yes. So you are. Then you know that I can easily keep you in the manner to which you've become accustomed."

"Okay."

"You're happy to be a kept man?"

"As long as it's you that's doing the keeping."

"What's all this rubbish about forgetting our engagement then?"

"I didn't want you to feel obligated. And things are different now."

"That's true – there is a dog to be taken into account now. He was never in the equation was he? I can't expect you to take on responsibilities you never asked for."

"No, indeed."

"I'm not going to get rid of the dog. He's my dog now. He belongs with me. I know you don't really like pets."

"What makes you think that?"

"I remember what you were like with Belter. You didn't like him."

"He bit me!" Tom pulled up his sleeve to show a faint white scar and stabbed at it with his finger. He looked outraged. "Of course I wasn't going to be that relaxed around him. He didn't like me."

"Jeff-Dog likes you."

"Jeff-Dog likes everyone."

"That's true."

"You'll get hairs all over your suits, and as for your super-duper Jaguar…" she trailed off. "You could get another car," she suggested. "Something not so posh and super-duper…"

"I'm not getting rid of my Jag!" he said, affront in every line of his body.

"Oh. Well. Maybe it won't work, then." Grief threatened to close her throat and she could say no more. She wasn't going to give up her dog.

"Come with me," he said, holding his hand out to her. Jeff-Dog woofed and leapt to his feet sensing an escapade.

Tom led Kate to where his car was parked. As they approached Kate could make out something odd about the back seat. On closer inspection she could see a luxurious, padded, hammock-like structure that extended from the back of the front seats across the back seat and up to, and looped around, the head rests.

"It will stop Jeff-Dog from falling off the seat if I have to brake suddenly. It'll keep him safe in the car. There is also a harness if you think we need that as well. I wasn't sure."

Kate couldn't immediately speak. "You'd let Jeff-Dog in your super-duper Jaguar?" she croaked.

"Of course I would!"

Jeff-Dog jumped up and barked and Kate leapt in front of him in case he scratched the silver paint. She'd have to teach him *that* was a definite no-no!

"Where did you get it over the bank holiday?"

"I've had it for a couple of weeks. I got it when you first mentioned fostering a dog."

Kate looked at Tom and knew she would never, ever be able to get his ring off her finger. He was so absolutely perfect!

Fireworks from very, very late-night revellers lit the sky with an orangey glow and Jeff-Dog yelped and scrabbled madly to get past her. Without thinking she turned and opened the back door of the Jaguar and Jeff-Dog flew in as if propelled by turbine engines; he huddled in the far corner, fearfully peering back the way he'd come, his mortal dread erratically huffing from his open mouth.

Kate climbed in with him and pulled him onto her lap. More fireworks cracked the night, scorching the sky and, no doubt, frightening all the wildlife for miles around. Did they really have to be that loud? The other door opened and Tom climbed in. He had to sit lengthways because of the hammock contraption. He shifted both Kate and Jeff-Dog onto his lap. Once both doors were closed the noise abated and the car filled with the sounds of a panting dog, and heavy-breathing humans. The smell of expensive leather competed with the aroma of dog, the perfume of fresh laundry and Tom's aftershave. It was heaven.

Kate fit well on Tom's lap, while Jeff-Dog overflowed hers. Kate felt a bit sandwich-like. In a nice way.

"You're going to be covered in dog fur now," she murmured relaxing into Tom.

"I don't care. This is exactly where I want to be," he said into her hair.

"*You're* my hero," Kate said. "You're my real hero. I don't need any of that flowing cape and mask stuff. I just need you."

And even Jeff-Dog stopped trembling in the wonder and certainty of it all.

the end

Printed in Great Britain
by Amazon.co.uk, Ltd.,
Marston Gate.